I Am America

IF THE FIRE COMES

A Story of Segregation during the Great Depression

Book design by Jake Slavik
Illustrations by Eric Freeberg

Photographs ©: Library of Congress, 148 (top); "Pictorial Review: Sparta District, Company 605, Camp Skokie Valley, SP-15" (Glenview, IL: Civilian Conservation Corps, 1939), 148 (bottom); US National Archives and Records Administration, 149 (top); USFS photo #342636/Gerald W. Williams Collection/OSU Special Collections & Archives, 149 (bottom); North Star Editions, 150, 151

Published in the United States by Jolly Fish Press, an imprint of North Star Editions, Inc.

First Edition
First Printing, 2019

Library of Congress Cataloging-in-Publication Data
Names: Daley, Tracy, author. | Freeberg, Eric, illustrator.
Title: If the fire comes : a story of segregation during the Great Depression / by Tracy Daley ; illustrated by Eric Freeberg.
Description: First edition. | Mendota Heights, MN : Jolly Fish Press, [2020]. | Series: I am America | Summary: "Joseph McCoy plans a secret project to help save an all-black Civilian Conservation Corps camp from being forced out of town in 1935 Elsinore, California"—Provided by publisher.
Identifiers: LCCN 2019001047 (print) | LCCN 2019004295 (ebook) | ISBN 9781631633737 (ebook) | ISBN 9781631633720 (pbk.) | ISBN 9781631633713 (hardcover)
Subjects: LCSH: Civilian Conservation Corps (U.S.) | CYAC: Civilian Conservation Corps (U.S.) | Segregation—Fiction. | Prejudices—Fiction. | African Americans—Fiction. | Depressions—1929—Fiction. | Elsinore (Calif.)—History—20th century—Fiction. | LCGFT: Fiction.
Classification: LCC PZ7.1.D287 (ebook) | LCC PZ7.1.D287 If 2019 (print) | DDC [Fic]—dc23
LC record available at https://lccn.loc.gov/2019001047

Jolly Fish Press
North Star Editions, Inc.
2297 Waters Drive
Mendota Heights, MN 55120
www.jollyfishpress.com

Printed in the United States of America

I Am America

IF THE FIRE COMES

A Story of Segregation during the Great Depression

By Tracy Daley

Illustrated by Eric Freeberg

Consultant: Andrew Lee Feight, PhD,
Professor of American History, Shawnee State University

JOLLY
FiSH
PRESS

Mendota Heights, Minnesota

Chapter One

August 5, 1935
Mission: Save the Pigeons
Operative: Joseph McCoy

Summary:

It's been a week since I brought the pigeons home. They made Maya smile. The last few months since she's had polio have been hard. Her legs don't work right anymore, and she's been stuck in bed. There are two things that cheer her up: my spy stories and the presents I bring home—the pigeons being the best find so far.

I tell her the story every night to see if she'll smile again—how I knew the gambler, a pigeon racer, was down on his luck. I'd shined his shoes a dozen times, so I'd heard all his stories. I followed him five blocks without being noticed, sly as a real spy, and watched him dump his losing birds in the trash behind the mercantile.

Maya's favorite part is how I waited until he left and then saved the birds, bent cages and all.

I'd heard how pigeons can send messages, and I thought Maya and I could use them in our spy games, but something's wrong. The last few days, the pigeons have been lying down, not getting up when I bring them the leftover cornbread and milk. Maya says they are sick because we aren't feeding them right.

Today, I'm going to make enough money to get real pigeon feed. I might have to shine a dozen shoes to do it, but I'm not coming home until I can make the birds better. I worry that if something happens to the pigeons, Maya might never smile again.

*J*oseph McCoy could tell a lot by the shoes a person wore. Or didn't wear.

Uncle Tanner's shoes sat by the door of the shop Joseph and his family lived in, untouched on a weekday morning. Uncle Tanner's boots, a pair of Red Wings worn down to the metal over the toe, told the story of a man who'd worked hard once.

Shifting the boots to set his shoeshine box down by the door, Joseph could smell the oil and smoke from the leather. Uncle Tanner had been a metalworker before the Depression. He'd even been able to save up to have his own shop and tools, but he'd been out of work for almost two years now. His boots sat by the door more and more often. It was rare for Uncle Tanner to even come out of the back room now.

Joseph checked his shoeshine box, making sure his supplies were ready for the day: black liquid, polishing cloth, Griffin shoe polish, and several small brushes. Joseph was the best shoeshine in Elsinore, California. He knew how to get every detail right, and his hands didn't shake, steady and sure. He never got black on a customer's socks. Joseph could tell the difference between a movie star and an athlete, a businessman and a crook, or a banker and a lawyer.

"You leaving already?" Maya asked, making Joseph jump.

"I want to get an early start," Joseph said, walking across the shop to the side of Maya's bed. She slept out in the open; Joseph slept on the floor next to her. The shop only had one room in the back, where Uncle Tanner disappeared to more and more often.

Maya was two years older than Joseph, a ripe old age of thirteen, but she still liked to play their spy game. And even though she didn't get around the way she used to, she could talk all day, fix a clock without thinking, and pinch as hard as a crab.

Joseph was about to sit down next to her when he heard cooing coming from Maya's feet. Not again. He pulled the thin blanket up from the bottom and found Simon, Maya's favorite bird. He was nestled between Maya's crooked legs, thin as pencils. He could see a spot of blood on her ankles from where she must have dragged her legs across the floor.

"Simon wasn't feeling well. I wanted to keep him warm," Maya said, sticking her chin out in her stubborn way.

"Are you okay?" Joseph asked.

"Of course," Maya said, but Joseph saw her tuck her hands behind her back. She got slivers when she dragged herself across the shop, no matter how many times Joseph swept. Maya was hard to keep down.

Joseph reached down and patted Simon, the smallest of the seventeen pigeons, on the head. Beside the bird, Joseph saw the book they read each night, *The Thirty-Nine Steps*, which had been one of Momma's favorite spy novels. It helped them get in the mood for their game and keep life exciting for Maya. Their game was to pretend Joseph was going out on a spy mission, a shoeshine boy as his cover.

Joseph wanted to say more about Maya pulling herself across the floor to get to the pigeon cages, but Maya gave him one of her looks. She pushed herself

up to a sitting position, hanging on to the side of the bed for support. "I'll check the radio, in case a secret message comes through. You go see what you can find out from the contacts downtown."

They kept the radio close to Maya's bed so she could listen during the day. She'd read all of Momma's spy novels at least ten times over. They usually had fun playing spies, but Maya didn't smile today, and her voice was flat. She was just trying to get him out of the shop.

"What can I bring you today?" Joseph asked. "Maybe some peanut butter and crackers?" They were Maya's favorite, and she needed something to look forward to.

Maya hadn't been the same since Momma's heart had given out two years ago. Papa had died from influenza when Joseph was small, so him being gone was just a fact of life. But Momma . . . well, Momma's absence had left a huge hole in both their hearts, Maya's especially.

Uncle Tanner was Momma's only brother, and he'd been kind and understanding at first. But after Uncle Tanner had lost his job, things had changed. They'd had to move out of Uncle Tanner's house and into the shop where he used to work. It was mostly cleaned out now, the tools sold to keep them fed. Uncle Tanner's kindness seemed to dwindle with the sale of each tool.

All that was left now was the forge with the bellows, a brass blowtorch, and some hand tools hanging along the wall. It wasn't a large shop, but the emptiness made the space feel hollow.

"I need some wheels," Maya said, lowering her head to the pillow. "Maybe a bike. Bring me a bike." She gave him a sad smile like she was sorry for asking. "And the crown jewels of England."

"I'm a spy, not a thief."

"Yes, of course," Maya said, turning her head away from him. "A war hero. Go spy me some peanut butter and crackers."

Joseph resolved to shine enough shoes to get the crackers, food for the birds, and maybe a treat to go with it.

He slipped out the door of the shop and blinked at the bright morning sun. The shop was the last building on the south side of town, which might have explained why no one had bothered to kick Uncle Tanner out. Joseph liked the space on the edge of town. The large field behind the shop was flat and open, providing a beautiful view of the mountains.

Joseph walked through Elsinore, a couple miles to the center of everything. It was where the new city hall stood, tall and glorious, red brick with a dozen windows, built just last year. Uncle Tanner had tried to get a job to help build the city hall, but they had been hiring whites only. The Depression had made whites so desperate for work they were taking jobs they never would have done before, jobs that black people used to do. Now there was no work at all. If a white man applied, he got it first. Uncle Tanner had complained long and loud for a while, but lately he hadn't even bothered to make a fuss.

City hall was where the shoes were. Politicians and bankers, lawyers and crooks all came to city hall. It helped that the bank was right across the street. There was a crowd outside today, a buzz of news in the air, the kind of news that starts small and then spreads like a wildfire. This was just the place for a spy.

Chapter Two

"Shoeshine!" Joseph called out, setting his box up on the sidewalk. "Ten cents a shine! I'll have you cleaned and buffed in just a few minutes!"

A man slowed in front of him, his shoes scuffed slightly on the toe. Oxford wing tip. A government man, then, with influence in the court, whites only. A spy could get valuable information from a man like that.

"Could I offer you a shine, sir?" Joseph asked, looking up. The man had a woman with him. Joseph had seen her on other trips to city hall. She was a white woman who spoke with more authority than the mayor. Mrs. Shirley Bailey.

The man put his foot up on the box. Mrs. Bailey's blue-suede shoes stopped beside him.

"I can't believe this is happening," Mrs. Bailey said. She tapped her high heel. "They're sending that segregated camp right here to Elsinore. There are plenty of other work-camp locations in California. They should send them somewhere else. If we truly have need of a CCC camp, give us a different one."

"It's the army's decision," the man answered.

Joseph finished the buff on the man's shoe and pulled out the shoe polish. The smell reminded him of paint. If he didn't have to be a spy shining shoes, he'd be using his steady hands as an artist, painting a picture instead of avoiding putting spots on a sock.

The man continued. "I don't know why they decided to segregate all the camps. They've been mixed until now."

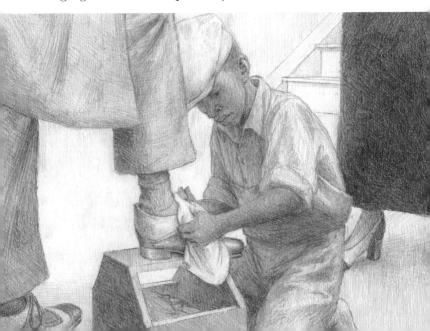

Mrs. Bailey made a huffing noise like she could tell an army which way to march. "I don't know why the change either. Heaven knows we're far more civilized than the South."

There was a pause and shift in the adults above him. Joseph focused on buffing the toe real good. He had a feeling they were looking at him, which could mean his spy cover was blown.

Mrs. Bailey continued in a loud whisper, like she was showing respect for the dead. "I don't mind them here and there. We have a few in town, and I'm liberal. No need to segregate a few. But when it's a whole camp of them, over one hundred fifty, what's that going to do to our community? We already have our hands full dealing with migrants and homeless coming through looking for work. "

Joseph finished the man's second shoe in record time. Spy or no spy, he'd had enough of this conversation. He'd heard of the Civilian Conservation Corps last year. Posters had gone up all over town of white boys without shirts and healthy-looking muscles: "A Young Man's Opportunity for Work Play Study & Health." The CCC was for eighteen-to twenty-five-year-olds only, so not an option for him or for Uncle Tanner. Joseph had checked.

The man threw Joseph a dime, and he and Mrs. Bailey moved off together.

Joseph shined several others' shoes that morning: a judge, a banker, and the owner of a hotel near Lake Elsinore. They all talked about the upcoming arrival of the newly formed CCC camp and the troubles that might arise from a camp so close to the town, though none of them actually said what kind of trouble they were expecting.

Just before lunch, Joseph had enough money for Maya's peanut butter and crackers and some milk for the morning, but he needed one more shoeshine to get ten cents' worth of pigeon feed from the mercantile. He called out to a few men, but this late in the morning, they all seemed to be hurrying to get to somewhere important.

That's when Joseph saw The Shoes.

Chapter Three

Joseph the Spy had to follow The Shoes. They were a pair of Bostonians, only worn a few times, the shine barely dimmed by a layer of dust from walking down the street. It wasn't so much the shoes that grabbed his spy senses; it was the rest of the man who went with them.

Everyone knew about Mr. Healey, but he rarely came into town. He lived on the west end of Elsinore and was rumored to be crazy. Joseph had heard that he'd served in the Great War and had lost his mind in the fighting.

Mr. Healey and his shoes didn't fit into any category Joseph could think of. The shoes were practically brand new, not even wearing through on the toes. Yet Mr. Healey's pants, shirt, and bearded face didn't match up.

His pants and shirt were threadbare and had holes in the knees and elbows. His shoulders sagged like he carried flour bags in both hands, and his beard hadn't been trimmed in a good long while. With the exception of his shoes, Mr. Healey looked like all the rest of the poor white folks who came into town from Hooverville, the cardboard city where homeless travelers lived in tents and lean-tos, a lot of them farmers who had escaped from the Dust Bowl in Oklahoma. They drove by the shop, sometimes in lines of ten or more cars, coming into town loaded down with so much stuff and so many people that the tires barely held the cars off the ground.

Joseph never asked to shine their shoes. Can't make money from people who don't have any.

Strange or not, Joseph needed a customer, and Mr. Healey had shoes that called out for a shine. Joseph picked up his shoeshine box and darted across the street. He followed Mr. Healey around the corner and up another block.

"Hey, mister!" Joseph called. "Can I give your shoes a shine?"

Mr. Healey stopped and turned. He had been known to talk to himself, but Joseph had never been close enough to notice before. Now that he was, he regretted it.

Mr. Healey growled deep in his throat and leaned toward Joseph, almost like he wanted to bite off his head. Joseph took a step back before remembering his mission. He needed money to feed the pigeons. It was now or never.

"I'll make those shoes shine like new. Make you look real professional." Joseph knew how to sell to white men in their fancy shoes, but all of his usual pitches seemed to fall flat in the face of Mr. Healey's scowl.

Mr. Healey started to turn away.

"Wait." Joseph couldn't give up, growl or no growl. He dropped all his shoeshine lines and just looked Mr. Healey straight in those washed-out blue eyes. "Please." Joseph swallowed. "It's important."

One of Mr. Healey's eyebrows went straight up. Then, in a miracle that Preacher Daniels would have talked about on Sunday, Mr. Healey nodded. Hot dog! Joseph would save the birds after all.

Joseph placed his shoeshine box on the ground and pulled out his black liquid, brushes, and polishing cloth. Mr. Healey lifted one foot onto the box, and Joseph applied the cleaning liquid with a little brown brush. When Joseph got to the polishing step, Mr. Healey started mumbling. Not to anyone. Not in words Joseph could understand. Just a low murmur that tumbled around Joseph's head like clothes in one of those electric washing machines.

The rumors were true. Mr. Healey was off his rocker.

Just as Joseph began to apply the polish, the sound of grating gears pulled his attention away from his work. He looked up to see a line of army trucks, over a dozen, moving down the street like a military invasion. Some trucks had open beds, while others had canvas coverings. Three dark letters were printed across the canvas: CCC.

Mr. Healey's foot came off the shine box. He turned and shook his fist at the passing trucks, his mumblings turning into a tirade of words Joseph knew Momma would have had him sucking on soap for saying. When the trucks passed and Mr. Healey put his foot back on the box, the mumbling continued. Joseph didn't say anything as he finished the shine and accepted Mr. Healey's dime.

"Thank you, sir," Joseph said. Momma would have never let him walk away without showing his manners.

Besides, Joseph was curious. And when a spy was curious, he got answers. If Joseph politely said goodbye, Mr. Healey would never suspect he was about to be followed.

Chapter Four

August 5, 1935
ELSINORE DAILY CHRONICLE

SOUTHERN CALIFORNIA
BURNING

The temperature over the last two weeks has hit an all-time high. No rain for over three months has left this agricultural paradise dry and dying. While so many people are suffering from lack of work, the weather drains resources even further. Last week, over 500 workers were laid off because the peach crops had dried up and there weren't enough to pack and deliver.

Workers aren't the only ones feeling the heat. Another fire has ravaged the forest northeast of Cleveland. CCC workers from several camps were called in to help fight the fire. The fire claimed the lives of two workers and left seven in the hospital.

"There is too much fuel and not enough water," said Fire Chief Stanton. "We need better communication and quicker response times."

Lake Elsinore is at the lowest level recorded. Mayor Crown is asking for concerted efforts to conserve water throughout the region.

*J*oseph read the newspaper article while standing across the street from the mercantile. He'd followed Mr. Healey from the post office to the bank and now to the mercantile run by Mrs. Jackson. Mrs. Jackson was the only woman, and black person, Joseph knew who owned her own store. And she wore sensible shoes, Star lace-ups. Joseph felt proud whenever he thought about how she had come straight from the South on the Union Pacific Railroad with nothing but the clothes on her back. Rumor was, after her husband had been killed in the Great War, she'd went and got a loan from Al Capone himself and outsmarted the gangster before he went to Alcatraz.

Joseph didn't believe everything people said. He'd heard enough untruths while shining shoes to know fact from funny, but he liked to imagine Mrs. Jackson facing down the mob. She had that look that made a kid go straight to saying prayers of forgiveness before even thinking of swiping a penny candy.

She'd even thought of a system to stay open while the Depression ate up just about every other business, trading supplies for government rations for people who couldn't pay with money.

Joseph slipped inside the mercantile a few seconds behind Mr. Healey and pretended to study the magazine rack.

"Good day, Mr. Healey," Mrs. Jackson said, standing up from stocking the lower shelf in her display case.

"Morning, Laila," Mr. Healey responded. Joseph almost knocked over the magazine rack. No one called Mrs. Jackson by her first name. Not even the sheriff. Joseph had seen Mrs. Jackson tell off just about everybody in the county, and he moved around the rack to avoid Mrs. Jackson's wrath.

But Mrs. Jackson didn't even flinch. She just smiled and pulled a newspaper from the stack beside the register and handed one to Mr. Healey. Was Mr. Healey scarier than Al Capone? But Mrs. Jackson didn't look scared.

"Mighty dry and hot today. Can I interest you in a cold soda?"

"No," Mr. Healey said. "If we don't get some rain soon, we'll all be in a world of hurt. Last I heard, we lost half the artichokes to the drought." Mr. Healey spoke the words stiff and uneven. Like he'd tried to paint them on the back of his hand and couldn't quite read his writing.

Mrs. Jackson nodded like she did when Preacher Daniels talked about the sin of pride.

Joseph didn't much mind about the artichokes. It was one thing he couldn't stomach, even if it was the only thing he had on his plate.

Mrs. Jackson tapped on the front of the newspaper.

"I read about those CCC boys," Mrs. Jackson said. "Is your son out there fighting fires? Is he doing okay?" Those words felt real, like Mrs. Jackson was trying to get Mr. Healey to relax.

"Nope, he went north." Mr. Healey didn't expand any, even though he was talking about his son. "Did the shoes come in?" he asked.

Mr. Healey went and jumped subjects like a frog on a sinking lily pad. Joseph didn't know how many times he could be surprised today. Didn't Mr. Healey already have shoes on his feet?

Even Mrs. Jackson, who never showed her thoughts on her face, glanced over the counter at Mr. Healey's brand-new-shoe-covered feet. "Yes, sir. They arrived yesterday. Would you like them wrapped?"

"No."

Not even a "No, ma'am." Momma would have never let Joseph get away with manners half as bad as Mr. Healey's.

Mrs. Jackson pulled a pair of brand-new shoes, the same exact ones Mr. Healey wore, from behind the counter. Joseph let his jaw drop as Mr. Healey grabbed the shoes and set twenty-five dollars down on the counter. Twenty-five dollars? Uncle Tanner's shoes had cost almost three dollars. A brand new bike cost seven dollars. What was so great about Mr. Healey's shoes that made them cost twenty-five dollars? And why in the world would he need two pairs?

Mr. Healey didn't even wait for any change or bother with a goodbye. He stuffed the newspaper into a back pocket with a letter Joseph had seen him pick up at the post office and walked out, tying the shoelaces of his new shoes together and hanging the pair over his arm.

Joseph wanted to see where he was off to. But first, he needed to buy the peanut butter, crackers, and pigeon feed.

"How's Maya?" Mrs. Jackson asked, taking his coins and raising an eyebrow at the pigeon feed. "You're not so down that you're feeding her this, now, are you?"

"No, ma'am," Joseph said, shoving his purchases into the shoeshine box. "It's for a project. A secret project."

Joseph was out the door before Mrs. Jackson could ask any more questions.

Outside, Joseph looked around for Mr. Healey. He thought he caught a glimpse and hurried after him. But when Joseph reached the corner, there was no sign of him. Joseph looked around, disappointed. How could Mr. Healey have disappeared so quickly? Joseph walked, searching the busy streets. He'd lost him.

Joseph found himself heading west, past the train station, past the pool hall, past where the sidewalk cut off.

The homes on this side of town were older, built before the turn of the century. He knew Mr. Healey lived west, but he hadn't planned on trying to find his house. There weren't very many people on the streets anymore. A couple of kids leaning against a fence watched him walk by. Joseph kept his head down. This wasn't a place for a shoeshine.

Joseph came to an old house. It looked like it might have been nice once, probably with two bedrooms and a full kitchen. But now it looked as if the Depression had sat on the house like an old hog. The shutters hung loose, and the paint was peeling away. The porch, for no good reason that Joseph could see, slanted sideways. The house looked saggy and broken, and the yard was filled with everything from small broken toys to car parts and old appliances. There were piles of broken items against the house, resting near the fence, and stacked in the middle of the yard.

Joseph stepped up to the fence. Was that a wheel? The rubber was peaking up from under a pile of wooden crates. Joseph leaned forward to get a better look.

A hand grabbed him from behind and spun him around. Joseph closed his eyes and waited for a cuff to the side of the head. His friend Raymond had been cornered in an alley downtown. Got roughed up real good.

But nothing hit Joseph. Nothing happened. The hand remained on his shoulder. Slowly, Joseph opened one eye and was shocked to be looking up into the face of Mr. Healey.

Mr. Healey scowled down at him. "Did you think you could get away with spying on a spy?"

Chapter Five

Joseph was too stunned to speak.

"You following me, boy?" Mr. Healey asked. He dropped his hand from Joseph's shoulder and folded his arms, almost like he was disappointed he had to explain the business of a spy.

Joseph could see each line across Mr. Healey's forehead and the hairs that stuck straight up out of his bushy eyebrows. Mr. Healey had that familiar sunken-cheek look of someone who ate just enough to keep alive.

Joseph tried to get his mind to think straight, but he could only think of one thing.

"You're not a spy," Joseph finally managed.

"I caught you, didn't I?" Mr. Healey said as he rubbed his beard.

Joseph glanced at the shoes on Mr. Healey's feet and knew it couldn't be true.

"You can't be a spy," Joseph said, shaking his head.

"What makes you say that?" Mr. Healey asked.

"No spy would wear shoes like that. They make you stand out too much. Plus, we're not even at war."

Joseph thought he saw the side of Mr. Healey's beard lift a fraction of an inch. Could that be a smile?

"It was a long time ago," Mr. Healey said. "Haven't been much of a spy since the war, but I could still pick you out of a crowd. Hiding behind newspapers. Studying magazine racks. You've got a lot to learn if you want to be a spy."

"I know all about spying," Joseph said, forgetting about manners and the fact that he was talking to an elder and a white man. He should have kept his eyes down, but he was too excited. "I'm reading *The Thirty-Nine Steps* with my sister, and we finished *The Secret Agent* before that. Maya's an inventor. Once she grows up, she'll probably invent spy gadgets."

Joseph was shocked at himself, but the words tumbled out like they were chain links on an anchor and there was no bottom to the ocean.

"Spy gadgets?" Mr. Healey grunted. "Spying can be a dangerous job. I'd keep my nose in my own business if I were you."

Joseph had questions inside that were as hot as a potato straight out of the oven. He had to get them out, or they would burn him.

"What kind of a spy were you? Did you ever get shot? Did you ever kill anyone?"

Mr. Healey stared Joseph down and then walked past him, through the gate of the house they were standing in front of.

"Is this your house?" Joseph blurted.

Mr. Healey turned around. He nodded and rolled his eyes. "You pick things up quick."

Joseph looked around the yard. It seemed like it was full of treasure. Not clean treasure, but pieces of everything Joseph could imagine, collected and forgotten, calling out to him. There was a broken record player, dusty and worn. Maya could probably fix it. He saw a kitchen sink broken in half, a pile of empty soda cans, a car door. And that wheel.

"This ain't an art gallery. Get a move on." Mr. Healey moved to turn away again.

"Why do you have so much stuff?" Joseph asked. A spy needed information. Joseph couldn't leave until he'd gotten everything he could learn.

Mr. Healey took a deep breath. "I started a collection when I got back from the war. The neighbors don't like it much, but they don't see past the junk to the true value."

Joseph thought of Maya. She had so much to give, but people just couldn't see past the broken part, especially Uncle Tanner.

"Is it for sale?" Joseph asked.

Mr. Healey squinted at Joseph. "You got money?"

"No." He'd spent it all on crackers and feed. "Could I have the wheel? It's for my sister."

Mr. Healey glanced at the wheel. "What is your sister going to do with a wheel?"

"I don't know. She's laid up in bed, and my job is to get something to make her smile. Each day, I find something that helps. She had polio, like the president."

Mr. Healey shook his head. "I didn't know your kind got polio. Thought it was only . . . Never mind."

Does he think only white people get polio? White people always seemed to think they were the only people who got anything.

Mr. Healey's eyes were distant, his eyebrows pulled together. He looked sad. "Lost one of my boys to polio," he said, "and another to liberals."

Joseph didn't know what liberals did to people, but Mr. Healey made it sound as bad as polio. "Sorry, sir," Joseph said.

"If you manage to find a way to pull that wheel free, it's yours." Mr. Healey turned and went into his house without another word.

Joseph got to work shifting things and pulling on the wheel. It was stuck. He moved a rubber hose, a wooden pallet, and a heavy iron pot that might have been used for moonshining before Prohibition had ended. He pulled on the wheel again, but it was caught on something else. Losing patience, Joseph shoved and pulled and shoved some more. Finally, the wheel came, but not by itself. It was attached to a bicycle frame . . . and a second wheel.

It was a Black Beauty Schwinn. Broken, of course. The handlebars weren't attached, and the chain was rusted so bad the back tire wouldn't move, but the wheels were straight and solid.

This would definitely make Maya smile!

Joseph bent to pick up his shoeshine box when he noticed a newspaper in with his supplies. The front page was folded out, and Joseph saw that some of the letters were circled in black ink.

Someone had left him a code. A real-life secret message!

Chapter Six

I know about the birds.

That's what the secret message in the newspaper said.

Joseph walked home slowly, practically dragging the bike behind him on account of the rusted chain.

There was something else on his mind too. Tucked inside the newspaper with the secret message was a letter addressed to Mr. Healey. So it must have been Mr. Healey who sent the secret message. But how did he know about Joseph and Maya's secret project? Why did he care? And more importantly, what did the letter say? It was already opened, and Joseph knew he should return it. Still, Joseph wondered if a spy would return it without ever reading it . . .

Joseph shook his head. *What would Momma think if she knew I read a man's personal letter?* He had stuffed the letter into his shoeshine box to deal with later, but now he was having a hard time keeping his mind off it.

Joseph was almost home when the sounds of hammering, yelling, and clattering metal made it impossible to think. The usually quiet street was noisier than the courthouse before a trial. Joseph stowed the bike next to the front door and covered it with an old blanket that he found behind the shop. Then he put his shoeshine box on top of the covered seat and walked toward the sound to see what was going on.

The field that had stood empty this morning was busy as a beehive. The CCC trucks were parked in a neat row, right off the road. Dozens of workers were unloading the trucks while a whole swarm of them were setting up large canvas tents, pointed at the top and wide and square at the bottom.

Voices floated in the air, talking and laughing, along with the sounds of hammering and sawing. So that's what Mrs. Bailey had been talking about. The CCC camp was right outside the town. Right next to his uncle's shop.

Joseph's spy instincts kicked in. He dropped low and worked his way around the field, darting behind shrubs for cover. While the field was open in the middle, it was lined with scrubby sagebrush and thick grass bunches that covered the ground all the way up the mountain. There was plenty of cover for an eleven-year-old spy to stay out of sight.

At his vantage point, low to the ground, Joseph got a good look at the workers' shoes. The shoes of the workers moved back and forth, none of them calling out for a shine. These were work boots and military shoes, mostly. Thorogood and Brogue, some Red Wings like his uncle had. All the boots were dusty and worn, but sturdy, with life left in them.

And unlike the shoe owners in Elsinore, these shoes were worn by black people. Joseph had never seen so many black people all in one place—there must have been at least one hundred. On Sunday, Uncle Tanner used to take them to the African Methodist Episcopal Church down on Second Street, but it was only a congregation of about twenty. Pastor Daniels called them his flock.

On the west side of the camp, Joseph saw a group of workers standing at attention as if they were in the army. Mrs. Bailey had been wrong about the workers. While all of the workers in line were black, the uniformed man barking orders at them was white.

Joseph couldn't hear what he said, but each time he talked, a few of the workers would salute and move off toward another area of the camp.

Joseph wanted to keep watching, but it was getting late, and Maya would be wondering where he was. Plus, he'd brought home the bike. He might as well give it to her. The Black Beauty was sure to bring a smile. Wasn't it?

Halfway back to the shop, Joseph caught sight of a worker sitting outside one of the tents, drawing on a piece of paper. The worker's back was to Joseph, and Joseph could make out some dark lines under a large blue space on the worker's paper.

Quietly, Joseph crept as close as he dared, hiding behind the nearest sagebrush tree and leaning out to get a better look. Mountains. The worker was drawing a mountain scene with pastels.

"George!" another worker called out.

Joseph ducked behind a large branch.

"The captain wants you," the worker said to George. "Says he's got a special project with your name on it."

George stood, turned, and stretched, pausing for an instant when his eyes landed on Joseph's cover. Joseph scooted lower until George turned away.

"What's Captain got up his sleeve this time?" George asked. "That pine-beetle control project sounds special."

"How about finding a way to contain that wild elk herd?" Both workers laughed.

"Let me put my stuff away, and I'll be right there." George bent over and picked up his pastels and paper. The other worker walked off.

Joseph could hardly breathe. He'd never met another artist. Joseph peeked over his branch and found George staring right at him.

Losing his nerve, Joseph ran all the way back to the shop.

August 1, 1935

Dad,

I know you said not to send the money, but it's a requirement. We get paid $30 a month, and $25 has to go home to our families. That's you.

I was thinking about how you told me that the government claiming land as protected forests is a waste of resources. Sure, letting loggers and miners work these lands would create jobs, but if you could be here, I think you might get a vision for what the Roosevelts are talking about. There is a beauty here, away from people, that changes a man.

You've always taught me to take care of myself, not to depend on others. The CCC was the only way I could think to help myself. There are no jobs. But this is a real job. With real money. And I can't sit around and watch people waste away. I want to do something.

We've built trails and phone lines. We're working on one of the longest fire lines in the country. It could save hundreds of lives if there's a fire along the mountains. Dad, I'm not sorry for leaving. I just want you to understand.

Please write back.

Your son,
Henry

P.S. When there's an argument in camp, our commander has us put on boxing gloves. I went up against a kid named Langly Fields. One of the best boxers in our group. He could be the next Joe Louis. He left two days ago, along with the three other blacks in camp. Guess they got reassigned.

Chapter Seven

When Joseph came around the front of the shop, he saw that the door wasn't closed tight, a slight strip of light showing. The old blanket was still there, covering the broken Black Beauty, but his shoeshine box was gone.

"Maya!" Joseph yelled as he rushed through the door. He almost tripped as his feet hit a large obstacle just inside the doorway.

It was Maya.

"What are you doing out of bed?" Joseph asked, wishing he could have worked in more of the worry than the anger that had come out.

"I heard you outside, but when you didn't come in, I got scared." Maya shifted toward him, Mr. Healey's letter in her hand. "I thought you'd left me a secret code in your shoeshine box, but it was a letter. A real letter." She held it up to show him. "Is this the real Mr. Healey? The crazy one they used to talk about in school?"

Maya's eyes squinted, and she looked away after she said the word "school." Missing school was one of the things that made Maya the saddest. Joseph never talked about it, and he didn't mind that he was too busy shining shoes to sit at a desk, listening to teachers droning on. He liked learning but had no patience for school.

"Yeah," Joseph said, answering Maya's question about Mr. Healey. "I shined his shoes today and followed him home."

Maya pushed herself up. Joseph noticed a new scrape on her wrist. "You spied on Mr. Healey? Why?"

Joseph shrugged. "He was wearing new shoes." Did he need another reason to spy? "Come on. Let me help you get back in bed."

"I can do it." She pushed Joseph's hands away and began dragging herself back across the floor.

Joseph hated to watch her. He could see the pain in her face even through her determination. Joseph picked up

Mr. Healey's letter to put it back in the shoeshine box that Maya had pulled just inside the door.

He tried to fold it up without reading it, but he noticed the date on the top and the signature on the bottom. "This letter is from his son!"

Maya reached the edge of her bed. She grabbed the railing and pulled. She shifted, wriggling like a worm until she had enough of her body on the bed to roll over. "You sound surprised. Who else would write Mr. Healey?"

"But he told me his son was dead."

Maya didn't lift her head from the pillow. "Are you sure?"

"Well, he said he lost one son to polio and one son to liberals." Joseph put the letter in the shoebox and walked over to Maya. "What kind of a disease is liberals?"

Maya laughed, putting a hand over her face. "Liberals isn't a disease. It's people who want to change the way things are. Make things different. Like President Roosevelt and the First Lady." Joseph knew Maya listened to Eleanor Roosevelt on the radio every week.

"Then why aren't things getting better?" Joseph asked, surprised at the anger he suddenly felt. "Why can't Uncle Tanner get a job? Or any of the men from church?"

Maya's eyes looked down, focusing on her legs. "Wanting things doesn't always make them happen."

Before Joseph could think of what to say, the door to the back room opened and Uncle Tanner came out. Uncle Tanner wore a dirty white T-shirt and too-loose pants held up by a belt tightened on handmade holes. He never lifted his eyes from the floor.

"Did you get any food?" Uncle Tanner asked gruffly. "Gotta do something to earn your keep around here."

Joseph stood quickly, moving back to his shoeshine box and pulling out the peanut butter and crackers. "I earned enough for this." Joseph held them up like an offering. Uncle Tanner often talked about how he had no ability to care for kids. Not enough money. Not even a decent place to live. On his bad days, he talked about selling them for one meal of biscuits and gravy.

"Peanut butter and crackers?" Uncle Joseph shuffled closer, just enough to see the offering in Joseph's hand without lifting his eyes to meet Joseph's. "What kind of a dinner is that? You could have got some corn meal and oil for the same price and had it last two weeks."

This was one of Uncle Tanner's bad days.

"Might as well eat those birds." Uncle Tanner shot a look at the six cages in the corner of the room. The pigeons were listless, lying around like boneless chickens. Joseph needed to get them their new bird feed. And convince Uncle Tanner that peanut butter and crackers were better than roasting the pigeons over a fire.

"Don't you dare," Maya said, loud and firm, sitting up straight. "Those are special birds. You can't eat *these* pigeons."

Joseph held the crackers and peanut butter up as a peace offering to Uncle Tanner. Uncle Tanner opened his mouth and then looked away, clenching his jaw. Maya used to be his favorite. He'd work with her on his shop projects, teaching her welding and cutting. But he hadn't talked to her since her legs had stopped working. Hadn't even looked at her in over six months.

Uncle Tanner grabbed the peanut butter and crackers and shuffled back to his room without a word.

When Joseph looked at Maya, he could see the blinks that held back her tears. They both missed the old Uncle Tanner. When he'd had a job, he'd laughed a lot, brought them presents from the mercantile, and done crossword puzzles in the *Elsinore Chronicle*. Now it was as if the old Uncle Tanner had shriveled and rotted like an apple core in the sun.

Mrs. Jackson had told Joseph and Maya to be patient with Uncle Tanner. "Men need jobs," she had said. "They need to work with their hands and have a purpose. When they don't . . . well, sometimes they forget who they are."

Maya's sniffle brought Joseph back from his memory. But when he reached toward her, she waved him away. "Did you get the feed for the birds? At least Uncle Tanner didn't take that."

"Yes," Joseph said. Then he remembered his surprise. "And I brought you something else. I'll give the birds the food, and then I'll bring the surprise inside. Stay right there."

"Like I can go anywhere," Maya said, a small twitch at the cornerss of her mouth.

Later, when Joseph pulled the bike in, dragging it on the back tire that didn't spin right, he held his breath, but he shouldn't have worried.

The twitch that had started earlier spread into a full grin, showing the white of Maya's teeth.

"I brought you a tire!" Joseph announced.

"Joseph!" Maya said, the awe in her voice making Joseph want to blush. A broken bike wasn't that big of a deal. "You brought *two* tires! This is so much better than the crown jewels of England."

Chamber of Commerce Disapproves of Civilian Conservation Corps

Yesterday, the newly segregated CCC camp 2923 was assigned to a location near Elsinore, California. While CCC camps have been growing in popularity, some citizens of the community have come forward to voice their concerns.

"The City of Elsinore has the right to want high-class, safe, and responsible citizens. This new segregated CCC camp could bring all kinds of trouble to our town," said Mrs. Shirley Bailey, wife of the president of the chamber of commerce.

Camp 2923 consists of 150 black workers under the command of Captain Kenneth P. Jones. Their assignment will be to work on fire prevention and firefighting in and around Cleveland National Forest. They will also be assigned various projects such as telephone-line construction and beetle control.

Mr. Jay Newberry, a member of the chamber of commerce, said his main concern is to cultivate business and generate jobs for the citizens of Elsinore. "We need to make sure that the white men of this community have jobs. Those CCC workers are taking work that could be given to the locals who are in desperate need of employment."

California has 168 CCC camps. Five segregated camps were formed at the beginning of August.

Chapter Eight

The next day at city hall felt different. There was a static in the air that made the hair on the back of Joseph's neck stand up. He couldn't quite tell what was causing it until he tried to get his first few shoeshine customers.

"Get your shoes shined for just ten cents! Best shoeshine in the valley!"

One man stopped and looked at Joseph. Looked right at him!

Well, not exactly. There was no eye contact, but the man glanced at Joseph's face and hands. Then kept right on walking. Joseph studied his hands to see if he could tell what was different than the day before. They were his same old hands, a little shoeshine stain on his fingers.

Joseph shrugged off the strange feeling and walked to the other side of the street, a little farther from city hall. He called out to a couple of businessmen with matching

Sperry wing tips. Shoes for a business loan. Those were gimmie customers. They'd do anything to have a better chance with the bankers.

"Let me offer you two a shine," Joseph said, stepping in front of the men before they could go in the doors. "I'll get your shoes shining like new in no time. You'll have the best-looking pair of shoes in the bank."

The first man stopped, just the way they always did, and Joseph squatted down to get out his supplies. But the second man shook his head, lifting his chin toward Joseph, pulling the other man's arm to keep him walking.

They both looked sideways at Joseph and walked away. Yesterday, Joseph would have sworn he was invisible, spying and shoeshining without a soul in the world who noticed. Now he felt like he was glowing a strange sort of green.

What in the Sam Hill was going on?

Joseph tried a few more spots in town, but had the same result on each corner. After the sixth time he was rejected, Joseph kicked his shoeshine cloth and sat on the curb. This wasn't good. He'd never made a lot of money as a shoeshine, but he had always been able to bring something home for Maya and Uncle Tanner. His stomach was already growling double time from the missed dinner last night.

A flash from across the street caught his eye. It was Mr. Healey's shoes, again, shining like twinkling stars as they made their way through the crowd. Then the shoes stopped. Right across the street from Joseph. The people walking down the street shifted to walk around Mr. Healey. No one seemed to want to get too close. Joseph could see Mr. Healey's mouth moving and his hands twitching, his eyes locked on the sidewalk.

That's when Mr. Healey looked up and stared straight at Joseph. He wasn't the first person to notice Joseph today, but he was the first person to actually look at him. Eye to eye.

Then Mr. Healey did something very strange.

He pulled a paper out from his coat pocket and snapped it open like he was going to read it. Only his eyes never left Joseph's. Then Mr. Healey carefully refolded the paper, turned around, and walked through the crowd as if they weren't there, moving toward the movie theater.

There was a small line outside the theater, white folks with jobs waiting to buy tickets to *Call of the Wild*. Joseph had never seen a motion picture, but he wasn't wondering what it was like inside those walls now. He kept his eyes on Mr. Healey. With one final glance back at Joseph, Mr. Healey bent over and set the newspaper under the bench in front of the theater.

No one noticed. No one stopped. Mr. Healey didn't wait to see what Joseph did. He walked down the street, disappearing around the corner of the next building.

Joseph's heart was racing like he'd run a mile. Mr. Healey had said he'd been a spy in the war, but why was he acting like one now? Why had he made sure Joseph saw him hide the newspaper?

There was only one way to find out.

Joseph picked up his shoeshine box, waited for a car to pass, and then darted across the street to the bench in front of the theater.

He tucked Mr. Healey's paper under his arm and ran all the way back to the shop. If he was getting a message from an undercover spy, he had to share it with Maya.

When he'd left, Maya had been sleeping. But when Joseph got back, she wasn't in her bed. Before he could yell for her, he spotted her toward the back of the shop, slipping a piece of paper underneath Uncle Tanner's door.

"What are you doing?" Joseph asked.

"Shhh," she said, putting one finger against her lips. "Don't wake him up." She finished pushing the last corner of the paper under the door and then started pulling herself back toward the bed. Joseph knew that Maya's arms were strong. Once, when no one was looking, he'd tried to pull himself across the floor the way Maya did, without using his legs at all. He could hardly get himself to move.

"Are you playing spy games with Uncle Tanner now?" Joseph asked.

Maya smiled, shaking her head as she pulled her body forward. "No. I'm giving him something to do, something to keep his hands busy."

That didn't make a lot of sense. But before Joseph could ask her to explain, Maya gasped and stopped moving.

Joseph ran to her side. "What? Are you okay?"

"Fine." Maya tried to keep her hand behind her, but she couldn't keep her balance. When she put her hand back on the floor, Joseph could see the bloody blister that had popped on her palm.

"Here," Joseph said, keeping his eyes from looking at her hand. "Let me help. Just this once. I've got something to show you."

"What?" Maya asked, letting Joseph pull her arms up over his neck.

"We've got another message from the spy."

Chapter Nine

Care and Maintenance of War Pigeons

* Build them a loft—strong enough to keep predators out and a door to keep them in until they are settled. Keep the loft off the ground, and don't make a flat roof. Don't want the pigeons spending time on the roof. Make a trap door that lets the birds get in when they want, but only get out when you want.
* Give them fresh water daily. No milk.
* They need grain and grit. Clean up food twenty minutes after you feed them.
* Clean the floor of the loft every day.
* Teach them how to use the trap door.
* They can be trained to fly between different locations.

* *To train, start by taking them one mile away.*
Make sure they come home several times.
Then take them five miles. Then farther.
Carry them to release locations in a covered
cage or basket.

After only two days on a diet of water and pigeon feed, the pigeons were doing much better. Simon always came to the door first. Once, Simon had gotten out of the cage and flown around the shop until Maya had coaxed him back down with bird feed.

Joseph knew the birds probably wanted to be outside, especially now that they were feeling better. But Maya couldn't help care for them outdoors. And besides, what would happen if one escaped outdoors? Would it really come back?

"I would have never guessed milk would make the pigeons sick," Maya said. "I wonder how Mr. Healey knew we needed help?"

Joseph scratched an itch on the back of his head. It always seemed to itch there when he had a question he didn't know the answer to. He was glad the pigeons were feeling better, but now he wondered what Mr. Healey wanted in return. Maybe he was like those gangsters who did you a favor and then made you pay up when the debt came due.

He didn't have a lot of worry left for that problem. The shoeshining had gotten worse. Now, people didn't just ignore him; he'd been shoved out of the way and his supplies kicked to the curb. No one wanted a shine from him anymore. If it weren't for Mrs. Jackson bringing over some warm cornbread last night, they'd have gone hungry for the third day in a row.

Uncle Tanner hadn't complained. Instead, he'd taken Maya's bike.

Joseph couldn't believe it. He'd come out of his room the day before, Maya's paper in hand. He hadn't yelled at them, or spoken to them at all. He'd just taken the bike, and some welding tools that he hadn't touched in ages, outside. Probably to try and sell them, but he hadn't come home with any food.

Joseph couldn't let them go hungry one more day. He had a plan.

As a shoeshine, he knew he had to go where the money was, but right now, the wallets in town were shut tight. The only other place he knew for sure that there was money was at the CCC camp. Those workers had jobs. Most of them didn't need their shoes shined, but the officers might, or maybe he could do something else to earn a few coins.

Once he'd made sure Maya was comfortable in bed with some water to drink and the radio tuned to her favorite station, Joseph slipped outside and headed toward the field.

All of the tents were set up now—over twenty in total. They were all bigger than Uncle Tanner's shop, lined up in neat rows, evenly spaced. Joseph headed toward the closest tent, the one where he'd seen the artist, George.

It was early, and there were a few workers about, stretching, jogging in pairs. The morning smelled fresh, and there was a hint of bacon and syrup in air. Joseph spotted George outside his tent, pastels in hand. Joseph was only a few feet away when another worker came out of the tent, pulling on a shirt, suspenders hanging by his side.

"Any luck with Captain's special assignment?" the other worker asked George.

George lifted his head from his painting, eyebrows pulled together. "It's a strange request, Peter, that's for sure. Captain said no other camp in the state wanted the project."

"Why should we do it if no one else wants it?" Peter asked.

George stood up, setting his pastels aside and brushing the dirt from his pants. He hadn't put on any shoes yet, his bare feet seemingly as comfortable on the ground as Joseph's. "That's exactly why we should do it. We got to do something different. Something special. I think this project is just that opportunity."

Peter didn't answer George. He'd noticed Joseph. Joseph wanted to run, but he needed to get some kind of work. Maybe he could help with this special project.

"What have we here?" Peter asked as Joseph stepped closer. George turned around.

"I'm Joseph. I live next door." Joseph thumbed his hand toward the shop. "I'm the best shoeshine in Elsinore, but lately I can't get a single customer. I was hoping . . ." Joseph paused. He swallowed. He was brave enough to speak to these men. He had to sound more sure of himself. "I came to offer my services. See if I could help out around the camp."

George's lips turned up, but before he could respond, a horn as loud as a fire engine blared across the camp. Both George and Peter turned toward the sound.

"That's the fire call," Peter said to George. "Looks like your special project will have to wait."

"A fire?!" Joseph asked, alarmed.

Workers were coming out of all of the tents, flowing out like kids after a school bell.

"There's a wildfire someplace. It's our job to go help put it out," George explained. He bent over and put his pastels and paper into a pouch. "We've got to head out in the next half hour."

"You're leaving?" Joseph asked, hope for some extra change today sinking like a rock in his belly.

"Not for good," George said, rubbing the top of Joseph's head the way his father used to when he was small. "We'll be back as soon as we get the fire out. Maybe a day or two, maybe two weeks. That's the job."

Two weeks? Joseph couldn't wait two weeks.

"What about the special project? Is there something I could do while you're gone?" Joseph blurted. They had to give him something.

George paused.

Peter pulled up his suspenders. "There's no time to explain it, kid. We've got to get to the trucks."

George reached into his back pocket and pulled out an old, ragged wallet. "I got a strange request for you." George leaned over so he was eye to eye with Joseph.

Joseph stood up straighter, holding his breath in and pushing his shoulders back. He was getting a job.

"I need you to find me some pigeons," George added.

Joseph was so surprised, he blew out his air. "Pigeons?"

George pulled out two dollar bills. "I know it sounds weird, and I'll explain more later. But I'll give you two dollars now and three more when I get back, if you can get me ten or fifteen pigeons. Think you can catch some or something?"

Joseph took the two dollars, hands shaking. Was the world playing a prank on him? If so, it was a mighty good one. But the money was real enough.

"Yes, sir," Joseph said. George didn't even know that the job was already done. All Joseph had to do was convince Maya to sell the birds.

August 10, 1935

Mission: Spy Bird Training

Operative: Joseph McCoy

Summary:

Spies don't always agree. Maya and I have been arguing for hours about what kind of project a CCC camp would do that would need pigeons. Maya says they are run by the army, so of course they would need the birds to send secret messages. She has that look, though, a half smile with a crooked eyebrow, like maybe she might be teasing me.

I calmly reminded her that we are in California, and the only war going on is between workers and big business, but strikers don't need secret pigeons. The whole point of a strike is that everyone does it together, and everyone knows about it.

I admit I couldn't think of another reason for a CCC camp to need pigeons, but it doesn't really matter. I got $2 for food, and I'll be getting another $3 when they get back. Plus, they'll need someone to help take care of the pigeons. And I just happen to be a spy-bird-training professional! Well, I will be by the time George gets back.

Training begins tomorrow at 0800 hours.

Chapter Ten

*M*aya placed the cover over Joseph's shoeshine box. He'd emptied his supplies and left them under Maya's bed. Now the box held another secret project, one that cooed softly and smelled a little worse than shoeshine and paint.

They'd chosen to start the testing with Simon. Of all the birds, Joseph was most confident Simon would find his way home.

"Don't go farther than a mile. We don't want him getting lost the first time. And keep him covered until you are ready to let him go." Maya spouted directions like her voice alone could guide the pigeon home. She was extra nervous and kept glancing at Uncle Tanner's door.

Strange noises had been coming from his room. Banging and clanking, like he was taking his bed apart and jumping on the pieces. Joseph had knocked twice, but the noise had only stopped for a moment and then continued with no response.

"I'll be careful," Joseph assured Maya. "Everything will be fine."

Beside Simon, Joseph tucked Mr. Healey's letter from his son. He had to return it; the letter had been weighing on his conscience. That, and Mr. Healey had told Joseph and Maya how to train their pigeons. The least Joseph could do was return the letter Mr. Healey had accidentally left in the newspaper.

Joseph walked quickly, making sure the cover stayed even on the shoeshine box. Out of habit, he walked up past city hall and caught snatches of several conversations. He stopped and pretended to window-shop when he overheard a group of women talking about the CCC camp.

"It's because of the camp right outside of town," one woman said.

"My Gerald was laid off with the others yesterday," another said. "The terms of the strike were rejected, and they fired every single one of them. We need jobs in this town more than ever, and those black CCC workers are taking more than their share."

"I heard they're off fighting the Black Mountain Fire," a third woman said. "But they've been building phone lines and doing drought reconstruction all up and down the valley. Those are jobs our own men could be doing. Why should they have those jobs when our own husbands are out of work?"

One woman caught sight of Joseph standing near them. "Shoo," she said, waving her hand like Joseph was an annoying fly. "Get moving. We don't need your kind loitering on the streets."

Anger rose in Joseph's chest. These women didn't understand what they were talking about. It wasn't the CCC workers' fault their husbands didn't have jobs. He wanted to tell the women what he thought, but others had started to turn and stare. Joseph hated to be the center of attention. He turned, hurrying down the street to Mr. Healey's house.

When he got there, Mr. Healey was outside, sitting on his porch, staring at . . . nothing.

Joseph stepped through the gate and approached the man. At least he wasn't mumbling. He had the pair of brand-new shoes next to him, but not on his feet. His socks had holes big enough to see two toes on one foot and three on the other.

"Mr. Healey," Joseph started. "I wanted to say thanks. For helping with the birds, I mean."

Mr. Healey nodded reverently, like someone had mentioned a saint's name in a sermon. "Birds are a spy's best friend."

"Did you use them? Were you a trainer?" Joseph asked, information more important than manners at the moment. Momma wouldn't have been happy.

"Pigeons are so fast it's almost impossible to shoot them down. And they are more intelligent than a man. They never get lost. They can find their way through smoke, storms, and even in the dark."

Mr. Healey was talking to Joseph, but at the same time, he wasn't. Mr. Healey acted like the sky was listening to his story, and he would have kept going, even if there had been no one around.

Joseph shook his head. "Birds aren't smart. Hasn't anyone ever called you a bird brain? That's 'cause birds' brains are so small."

"Smart and brave," Mr. Healey argued.

"How can a bird be brave?" Joseph asked.

Mr. Healey acted like Joseph hadn't spoken. "The front lines are a scary place. There's fighting and dying. There are men, and there are guns. And it's always changing." He slowly tilted his rocking chair back and forth.

"See, a war pigeon always returns home," Mr. Healey continued. "You raise a pigeon where you want them to go, and then, when you take them far away, no matter how far, they return. In a war, armies use this to communicate. You put a message on the leg of the bird, and they take it back to headquarters."

Joseph found himself leaning forward. These were the most words he'd heard Mr. Healey speak. Mr. Healey might be a bit crazy, but he was a good storyteller. And his twitchy eye and scraggly beard made it feel like the story was coming straight from the source. Mr. Healey had seen war. Joseph could feel it in his words.

"During the war, a group of soldiers ended up surrounded behind the French lines. There was no way out. They hunkered down, but they couldn't last forever. One of the soldiers put the coordinates of their location on the leg of Cher Ami. That bird flew through a war zone, badly wounded, and delivered the coordinates. Saved almost two hundred men. Heroes. That's what you have: bird-brained heroes."

It was almost a joke, but Mr. Healey didn't smile or wait for Joseph to laugh. He got up and turned to go in his house.

"Wait," Joseph said. "I came to return this." Joseph held out the letter from Mr. Healey's son. "You left it in the newspaper with your first message."

Joseph thought for a moment and then added, "I thought he was dead, but I'm glad he's okay."

It was the wrong thing to say. Mr. Healey plucked the letter from Joseph's fingers. Before Joseph could blink, Mr. Healey ripped the letter into a dozen pieces and let the scraps scatter at his feet.

"Okay?" Mr. Healey's voice rasped with anger. "Is it okay to take borrowed money from a government that values trees over their own people? Save nature, sure, but the very vets who fought and died for their country aren't worth the slime on the bottom of their shoes. Being a traitor is worse than being dead."

With that, Mr. Healey went inside and slammed the door, leaving the pieces of his son's letter to swirl away with the wind.

Chapter Eleven

With Mr. Healey's outburst, the joy Joseph had felt that morning changed to sadness. He felt heavy inside. He carried Simon to the other side of Elsinore. He needed to put his conversation with Mr. Healey out of his mind. He had a mission to accomplish.

It was time to test the pigeon.

"It's only one mile, Simon. Not far at all, as long as you go the right way."

Pigeons didn't understand humans, but Joseph wanted Simon to make it. He wanted to tell George that not only had he found some pigeons but he had also trained them. He wanted to earn money for his family. He wanted Maya to be able to be free like a bird, not trapped in the shop all the time.

Joseph pulled the cloth off of his shoeshine box. Before he could grab Simon, the bird flew out of the box like his wings had already been flapping.

And worse, Simon was headed in the wrong direction!

"No, Simon!" Joseph yelled, motioning wildly with his arms. "That way. Fly that way."

There was no way for Simon to hear him, but Simon flew in a wide arch, adjusting his direction like a Great War plane coming in for a bombing. Mr. Healey had been right—pigeons flew fast and high. Before Joseph was sure Simon was going the right way, the small gray dot was out of sight.

Was the bird gone forever? Joseph stared at the blank sky for another moment before picking up the cloth and shoeshine box and running as fast as he could back home.

Joseph lost the race.

Simon was already there, sitting in the cage in Maya's lap.

But that wasn't even the most amazing thing. Maya was outside in the yard, holding the cage like she was about to present it to the First Lady herself, wearing a plaid dress

she hadn't put on since before she was sick and sitting in
Momma's old rocking chair.

Except the chair had wheels.

"We did it, Joseph!" Maya squealed, her eyes shining. "Simon is an official homing pigeon."

"What are you . . . What is that?" Joseph couldn't stop staring at the contraption that Maya was sitting in. It was a rocking chair without the rockers. It had a platform on the bottom for Maya's feet to rest on, two flat wooden feet, and wheels attached on either side with an axle.

"It's a wheelchair," Maya said, her voice full of pride. "Just like the president's. Well, not exactly, but it works the same." She paused. "Uncle Tanner built it for me, but I designed it."

"He did?" The world was tipping in a way that made Joseph feel dizzy. "Did he talk . . ."

Maya's happiness faded slightly from her face, and she shook her head. "I slipped the design under his door, and he left a note this morning that said it was outside. But he made it for me." She repeated the last sentence like it was the only truth in the world.

Glancing up, Joseph caught a flash of movement as the door to the shop closed, Uncle Tanner's face appearing for an instant in the opening before it was gone.

"Want to go to the mercantile?" Joseph asked. Mrs. Jackson's store had been Maya's favorite place, next to school.

"Do I!" Maya said. Not a question. "Put Simon inside and let's go."

Joseph made a move to push Maya's chair. "No," she said resolutely. "I can do it."

So the two of them traveled the three blocks to the mercantile. Maya stopped a few times as she got the hang of her new chair, but the smile never left her face.

Her chair couldn't fit through the door of the mercantile, but Mrs. Jackson came out with two glasses of ice-cold lemonade.

"Why, I never!" Mrs. Jackson exclaimed when she saw the chair. "Did your uncle make that?"

"Yes!" Maya said. "I gave him something to do to see if it would help, but he hasn't talked to me yet. He still won't even look at me."

Joseph had never heard Maya admit that out loud. She always acted like she didn't notice, but she had. And Joseph heard the hurt in her voice.

Mrs. Jackson placed her hand on Maya's arm. "Be patient with him. Your uncle is made of more than just himself."

"What does that mean?" Joseph asked.

"It means he comes from more than just what you see," Mrs. Jackson said. "He comes from a place where someone with a disfigurement isn't considered whole."

"You mean he sees me as half a person?" Maya asked.

"He'll learn how wrong he is. And this chair is a great start," Mrs. Jackson said. "We've all got a lot of learning to do."

Joseph wanted to ask about Mr. Healey. Maybe Mrs. Jackson could explain why he had ripped up a letter from a son who was still alive, but Joseph wasn't sure how to put it into words. It seemed like there was more learning to do than Joseph could manage in a whole lifetime.

Chapter Twelve

A week later, Joseph heard the roar of the CCC trucks pulling back into their camp. It was early afternoon, and Joseph and Maya had just put Simon back in his cage after his third successful return.

Joseph was so excited to tell George about Simon's success and get three more dollars that he barely had time to make sure Maya was back comfortably in her bed before he ran out the door. If he could convince George that he was the right person to care for the pigeons, maybe he could get a job for keeps.

When Joseph reached the camp, everyone looked exhausted and sweaty. There was a strong smell of smoke as the workers moved out of the trucks. Joseph paused when he saw George helping to pull a man on a stretcher out of the last truck.

"What happened?" Joseph asked, running up to help George. The worker in the stretcher was moaning. He had dirty bandages around his hands, and when he coughed, it sounded like his lungs were full of liquid.

George's face was grim. "We were fighting a fire up north. By the time we got there, the fire was out of control. We got in deep to try and make a fire line to the north, but the wind came up like someone had flicked on a fan. The fire changed directions and came straight for us. We got out, but a lot of us breathed in too much smoke. Charley here got burned."

Joseph helped carry Charley to the medical tent. No one stopped to tell Joseph to go home. They were all too exhausted to notice him.

"Is there anything I can do?" Joseph asked as he followed George out of the medical tent. "That sounds awful."

"Nothing any of us could have done," George answered, rubbing an already soiled handkerchief on the back of his neck. It just smeared the dirt and ash around. "The fire was too big before we even knew about it."

The sound of yelling from the road made Joseph turn around. A group of white boys from town drove past in cars, hanging out of the windows, throwing rocks and rotten fruit. The CCC workers closest to the road had to duck, but no one was hit. Everyone stopped and watched the cars go past.

"They really don't like us here," George said.

"They should," Joseph said. "What if we had a fire? No one in town would know what to do."

"If the fire comes, we'll be there," George said. "But for now, I'm going to get some rest."

"But I have the birds," Joseph blurted. "I've started training them. I'm the best pigeon trainer in the valley. And I was hoping . . ." Joseph felt bad pushing George right after the fire, but he couldn't wait. He really needed the job now. ". . . that I could help you take care of them. I don't know why you want pigeons, but I know how to help."

George didn't say anything for a minute, his mouth open just a little. "You got pigeons?"

Had George hit his head? Had he forgotten about the project?

"Of course," Joseph said.

George let out a long laugh. "That's amazing! I thought we'd have to order them or something, but now we can get started right away."

Joseph brushed at his sleeves like George's craziness was contagious. "Started on what?"

"Kid," George said, patting Joseph on the shoulder hard enough to knock him off balance, "together, you and I are going to save lives."

Chapter Thirteen

It was the last week of August, and the end of summer was hot enough to cook an egg on a rock. The dead grass crunched under their feet as George and Joseph took a step back from the new pigeon loft.

Nearby, Maya inspected their work. "This should work right," she said, pleased. "The hinge only goes one direction. The birds can get in, but not out."

"This was quite a design," George said. "You could be an engineer for Ford Motors someday."

Maya hid her face and mumbled something behind her hand. Joseph smiled, his happiness threatening to stretch the corners of his mouth right to his ears.

"That was a good day's work," George said after they had put the pigeons in their new home. "Let me get you two a soda in town. This calls for a celebration."

"You have to tell us what the pigeons are for," Maya said. She'd been bugging Joseph to find out, but Joseph had told her it was a top-secret project. He didn't want to admit he couldn't figure out what George would do with them.

"Well, Miss Maya," George said, "the state of California asked the CCC camps to train pigeons to carry messages as early fire warnings. The theory is that we'll be able to catch the fires before they get out of control."

"You mean you're not a secret government spy?" Joseph asked. He could always hope.

George belly-laughed, shaking his head. "Not yet. But maybe someday." He winked. "Come on. I'll get some of the boys rounded up."

Joseph watched the pigeons pecking around in their new loft. So they weren't going to be spy birds, but warning people about fires was a close second. Joseph was fascinated by George's stories about firefighting. How the firefighters communicated. Words like *fire line* and *wind shift*.

George walked next to Maya as they started up the sidewalk, talking about the last fire they had fought with a couple of the other workers who had helped build the loft. No one seemed bothered by Maya's wheelchair.

When Maya had pushed her chair into the camp with Joseph for the first time, there had been some strange looks, but George had treated Maya like a sister from the first instant. He had been the one who suggested Maya design the loft.

The group headed for the corner gas station. It had two pumps outside the building, a screen door, and an air-conditioned inside. Joseph liked to check out their candy selection until the owner kicked him out. The man was nice but didn't like local kids drooling on candy they couldn't afford.

Joseph followed George inside and ordered a cherry soda for himself and a Coca-Cola for Maya. As Joseph stepped outside to hand Maya her soda, he noticed a fancy Cadillac blowing smoke on the side of the road near the gas station. A man leaned over the smoking engine. Mrs. Bailey was yelling at the driver and waving a large fan in front of her face.

Mrs. Bailey stopped and marched toward the gas station. She must have yelled herself hoarse and needed a drink. She glanced at Joseph and Maya as she reached for the screen door. Just as she did, George pushed the screen door open, catching Mrs. Bailey square in the face. She toppled backward and landed on her rear end.

Mrs. Bailey's husband owned the cannery, the car dealership, and the theater, and she was chauffeured around in that Cadillac. She wasn't a woman you saw planted on her backside very often.

George jumped around the door to help her up. "I'm so—"

George didn't even get the "s" on "sorry" before Mrs. Bailey started screaming. George had taken her by the elbow to pull her up. Mrs. Bailey hit him with the big fan that was still in her hand.

A man who was pumping gas ran over and shoved George away. "Get your hands off her. What're you thinking, touching a white woman like that?"

Another white man ran out from inside from the store. He hadn't even seen what had happened, but he took a swing at George.

George took a hit to his right eye, but got in a right hook and made the man stumble. Joseph heard a yell from across the street as more men ran to see what was going on. One of the other CCC members was holding the arms of the second man behind his back, which the newcomers didn't take kindly to.

Before Joseph could blink twice, the whole parking lot of the gas station became a full-out rumble, men pushing and shoving, all kinds of shoes scuffing around on the concrete. And over it all, Mrs. Bailey was screaming her head off.

A shotgun blast echoed through the air. Everyone froze like someone had turned a motion picture into a still photo.

The owner of the gas station stood in front of his store, a smoking rifle pointed toward the sun. "I want everyone to just calm down."

One of the men took another step toward George, but the rifle leveled on the white man. "I mean it. Back off, everyone. I called the police, and they'll be here in just a moment."

It didn't take long for the police to show up. Mrs. Bailey wailed like a poorly tuned radio. The police listened to her first. George and the other CCC workers were lined up on the sidewalk and told to sit down until the police had finished investigating.

"How can the police do an investigation if they don't get both sides of the story?" Maya asked. She and Joseph had moved to the side of the building, away from the officers and Mrs. Bailey.

"Don't talk so loud," Joseph said. The last thing they needed right now was attention. "We're spies, remember. We can't blow our cover."

Without asking George or the other workers any questions, a police officer stood in front of them. "Because you are federal employees, we won't take you to jail, but you are banned from entering local establishments for the remainder of your stay here in Elsinore. We will escort you back to camp."

The workers were marched home, a police car following at a crawl, lights flashing. Another police officer helped a dirty, shaking Mrs. Bailey back into her Cadillac.

Joseph stood outside the now quiet gas station, everyone gone. The only evidence of the brawl was a single hat that rolled around in a circle, pushed by the breeze. Everyone had gone crazy so fast that not a single one of them had

had a minute to think. He didn't know why Mrs. Bailey had made such a ruckus. It had only been an accident.

Chapter Fourteen

September 5, 1935

ELSINORE DAILY CHRONICLE

CHAMBER OF COMMERCE MEETING

After the attack on her person, Mrs. Shirley Bailey has called for a meeting of the chamber of commerce to take place as soon as she returns from her recovery trip. After the traumatic experience at the gas station on Grahams Avenue, Mrs. Bailey has been suffering from the ill effects.

"I can't sleep. I can hardly eat. Every bone in my body shakes with fear for the safety of others in the community. While I want this issue taken care of right away, I need to take time to protect my own health," Mrs. Bailey said.

The purpose of the meeting will be to decide what to do about segregated CCC camp 2923 that has been assigned duty outside the city limits of Elsinore.

"It's the responsibility of the chamber of commerce to promote the welfare of the community," said Mr. Jordan Shirley, president of the chamber of commerce. "We will take this issue very seriously."

"There's only one solution, in my mind," Mrs. Bailey explained. "We've got to request the government remove them. We'll sign a petition and get that camp reassigned."

The meeting will take place on September 25 at city hall beginning at 7 p.m.

"That only leaves us three weeks to get the pigeons trained," Maya said.

"You think training the pigeons will make a difference?" Joseph tapped the newspaper with his finger. George's eye was still bruised from the fight, but Joseph wondered what injury Mrs. Bailey had to recover from.

"It has to," Maya said. "If they see that the CCC workers have developed a way to save lives, they will have to let them stay. They'll be heroes."

"Just like the birds." Joseph didn't say it loud enough for Maya to hear. The pigeons needed several weeks in their cage to realize where their new loft was. That didn't leave a lot of time for training at all.

"Maybe Mr. Healey has some tricks to help train them faster," Maya said. "We should go talk to him."

"He wanted to help us save the birds, but I don't think he'll help save the CCC camp," Joseph said. "He really doesn't like them."

"Why?" Maya asked.

"It has something to do with borrowing money," Joseph said.

The door to the back room opened. Joseph had been waiting for Uncle Tanner to come out for dinner. He and Maya had used their money from working with George to buy some real food: rolls and biscuits, with some gravy mix. Maybe Uncle Tanner would eat with them tonight.

"What's for dinner?" Uncle Tanner asked like a broken record player, like he couldn't think of any other way to start a conversation.

Joseph stood in front of the old cooking stove proudly. "Biscuits and gravy. I even warmed the gravy on the stove. Are you hungry?"

Uncle Tanner picked up one of the rolls sitting on an old work table. "Where did you get these? Who paid for them? Did you turn into a thief?"

"No." Joseph was surprised. He hadn't expected Uncle Tanner to get more angry when there was actually food on the stove. He couldn't think of what to say.

Maya spoke up. "We earned the money. We're helping the CCC camp across the street, and they pay us fifty cents a day."

Uncle Tanner's head twitched, like he had to force himself not to turn toward the sound of Maya's voice. "You have jobs?"

It was a quiet, desperate whisper that sent a chill of fear down Joseph's spine. He felt like there were a thousand answers the way Uncle Tanner had asked the question, but he could only think of two answers . . . and only one was true.

"Yes," Joseph said, hoping it would make Uncle Tanner proud.

Instead, Uncle Tanner's face crumpled in on itself. He took the roll in his hand and threw it on the ground. He kept his eyes on Joseph, but his finger pointed at Maya.

"You got a job. You. When I . . . when I can't?"

Maya shrank back on her bed. Joseph wanted to pull everything back, rewind, and start the moment again. What had happened? How had this special dinner gone so wrong?

Uncle Tanner just shook his head and walked out of the shop, leaving the door banging on its hinges.

Joseph picked up the roll and wiped the dirt off. No reason to let it go to waste. He made a plate for himself and Maya, and they ate in silence, listening to the sounds of the CCC camp that crept through the walls and invaded the shop. They were happy sounds of work and health that didn't belong in this room.

Finally, Maya put her food down. "We need to put a stop to this. We have to make this town see past their own noses."

Joseph nodded. Maya was right, but she'd seen the fight. She knew how quickly hate spread, like a wildfire on a mountain of dried-up grass. "What can we do? No one listens to kids."

"We need someone to help us."

"What about Mrs. Jackson?" She was the strongest person Joseph knew, besides Maya.

Maya shook her head. "I think it needs to be one of them. Someone white, but not blind."

"There's only one person in town who even still talks to me," Joseph said. "And he's kind of crazy."

Maya's eyes came up, the tears that had fallen silently while she ate dried on her cheeks. "We have to ask someone. Will you take a message to Mr. Healey? I'll write it in code. Maybe then he'll help us."

Joseph shrugged. "I'll take it, but I'm not sure he'll answer."

But a few days later, they did get an answer, hidden under the peanut butter and crackers Joseph bought at Mrs. Jackson's mercantile. It was an old newspaper article folded and refolded until the words on the creases had faded.

May 20, 1933

— The New York Daily Circular —

ROOSEVELT DOESN'T BEND FOR BONUS ARMY

Members of the "Lost Battalion," a group of soldiers who survived terrible conditions during the Great War behind the French lines, did not get the relief and change they had hoped President Roosevelt would give them. They came together with 1,000 other returned war veterans to ask President Roosevelt for an advance on their promised bonus bonds, but, like Hoover, Roosevelt will not approve the lump sum. The bonus bonds don't mature until 1945.

Most of the veterans have been out of work since the beginning of the Depression. Roosevelt, despite his promises of help and support for out-of-work and downtrodden citizens, denied their request. Roosevelt did offer work for many of the veterans in the Civilian Conservation Corps for one dollar a day, but refused to pay the promised bonuses.

This is the second Bonus March on Washington. The first march included 44,000 veterans and citizens. The army used cavalry and tanks to remove them from Washington. One veteran was killed, and 50 protesters and police officers were injured.

I cannot help when I am helpless

Chapter Fifteen

Joseph counted the birds again. Sixteen. He caught the one that had just flown into the loft through the trap door and checked the note in the small canister attached to the pigeon's leg.

"This one is Pigeon Thirteen. He was released from Menifee at 0900 hours."

Maya marked a chart on her lap. "Ten miles in fifteen minutes. Pigeon Thirteen was about three minutes slower than the others released from that location."

"No wonder that gambler kept losing his races."

Maya didn't laugh. She tapped her chart with the end of the pencil. Joseph knew why she was nervous. One pigeon was still missing.

"Simon will make it," Joseph told Maya.

Maya kept track of which pigeons made it home and how long it took them. George had given her a pocket watch, and Maya treated it like a jewel from the queen's crown.

Most of the birds had been trained for up to ten miles. Simon had made it the farthest so far.

Joseph and Maya had been helping the CCC camp train the birds for the last two weeks. Joseph liked to learn everything he could about firefighting while they were training the birds. He asked so many questions that some of the workers had started calling him Captain Curious.

Once the birds were ready, the CCC workers started taking the pigeons out on their assignments and releasing the birds from different locations, leaving the time and place in a message on the pigeon's leg. Joseph and Maya checked and recorded which birds came home and the time they arrived.

"They took Simon fifty miles today," Maya said.

Simon was ahead of the rest of the pigeons because they'd started training him first. This was the final test before the chamber of commerce meeting, and Maya and Joseph were going to show everyone how far the birds had gone.

If only the members of the chamber could see how useful the CCC camp was, they wouldn't send them away. Joseph was sure of it. He let out a whistle. "That's a long way. If he comes back, they have to listen to us. These birds will save lives. I have to convince them."

"You mean *we* have to convince them," Maya said. Maya had been insisting on coming to the chamber meeting so she could show the data. She said Joseph didn't know how to explain it well enough. Joseph knew it would be hard to get into the meeting with Maya's wheelchair, but they'd been planning ever since they'd gotten the note from Mr. Healey. "I wish George and the others could come."

Maya shook her head. "The captain is putting the whole camp on lockdown that night. He says he doesn't want any more incidences on his watch."

Joseph turned and kicked the empty feed bucket. "It's not fair. He should let them go. How can the people make a good decision if they don't get all the facts? George and the other workers won't cause trouble."

"I'm not sure it's the workers that the captain is worried about." Maya pushed her chair close enough so that she could put a hand on Joseph's arm. "It has to be us. We have to tell them."

"You're right," Joseph said. Then, with resolve, he asked, "Should we practice some more?"

Maya nodded, and the two made their way back to the shop.

They left the chair outside, since it didn't fit through the door, and Joseph helped Maya out of it. Once inside, Maya pulled herself to the side of the room where they had drawn marks with pieces of coal. "Okay. This is the alley where we leave my chair."

Joseph measured the distance from the shop door to the corner with his feet, taking even steps, even though he'd done it dozens of times. "It's exactly fifteen steps from the alley to the door of city hall. Once inside, I'll get you to the first available chair."

"Then, when the meeting starts," Maya continued, "you get their attention and tell them about the birds. Then I'll show them the data." She waved her clipboard in the air.

"Okay," Joseph said. The plan seemed simple, and they both knew the words by heart. But there was still the matter of getting Maya to the door.

So, every day for the last two weeks, Joseph had helped Maya practice going fifteen steps without her wheelchair. Maya had to lean on Joseph with most of her weight, her arm over his shoulder. And Joseph had to walk slow enough for Maya to pull each foot forward. It took her a lot of effort, and when she put weight on her legs, she would clench her jaw real tight. Even though most of her weight was on Joseph, the pain of putting weight on her legs showed all over her face. She wasn't walking, not really. It was more like being dragged gracefully. Joseph was glad he'd grown two inches this year and was almost as tall as his big sister.

Today, they almost made it to the door before Joseph stumbled, and Maya's legs gave out. They both crashed to the floor.

"Let's try again," Maya said.

"Do you want a break?" Joseph asked.

Maya shook her head. "We have to get it right."

September 25, 1935

Mission: Infiltrate Chamber of Commerce Meeting

Operatives: Joseph McCoy and Maya McCoy

Summary:

Simon came home at 1400 hours. He flew 50 miles in 50 minutes. The project is a success! Now we just have to convince the people at the meeting.

We are going to save the CCC camp.

Maya has all of her papers, her data, to show how the pigeons fly. I'm going to tell the people at the chamber meeting about George. He's smart, and he's an artist. Who wouldn't want to have a neighbor like that? Maya says they have time during the meeting for citizen comments, and they have to give us a chance to speak.

The one big problem is getting Maya into city hall. Uncle Tanner built a mighty fine wheelchair, but it doesn't fit through doors. We've got to get into the meeting and make them listen. We've been practicing, and we're both getting stronger. We made it 15 steps twice yesterday without falling.

The CCC camp has to stay. I haven't seen Maya smile this much since she got sick. I have a job. Things can't go back to the way they were. They just can't.

Chapter Sixteen

The crowd outside city hall was lined up like kids for a carnival ride. Joseph paused across the street, and Maya stopped her wheels next to him.

Maya had handwashed Joseph's old shoeshine shirt and her plaid dress until Joseph was sure she'd scrub them to nothing. She'd gotten some soap from Mrs. Jackson, and they both smelled like flowers. Joseph didn't think that would help their cause much.

"We didn't count for standing in a line," Joseph said.

"Look," Maya said. "It's Preacher Daniels and Mrs. Jackson."

Joseph looked and saw men and women from the African Methodist Episcopal Church being blocked from entering city hall. A crowd was forming behind them, making the line grow longer each second.

"They're not letting them in," Maya said. "We'll have to wait until everyone is inside. Then maybe we can sneak in."

"Just like spies," Joseph said, trying to ignore the nervous weight that sat at the bottom of his stomach.

Joseph turned to move farther down the sidewalk, but bumped straight into something, nearly falling backward from the impact. An older white boy stood in front of Joseph, hands on his hips. His lips were thin as a line. His shoes were straight from the Sears Roebuck catalog.

"Excuse you," the boy said. "Watch where you're going."

Joseph knew to keep his eyes down and move away, but Maya pushed forward. "You should watch where *you're* going."

The boy and three other boys behind him turned their attention on Maya. She hadn't had as much experience in the field as a spy. She didn't know how to stay invisible. Right now, she was the center of attention.

"What's that you're sitting on?" asked the biggest boy. "It looks like something from the junkyard."

"Look at her legs," said another one with hair so blond it looked like it glowed under the light of the street lamp. "They look like shriveled raisins!"

Joseph was so hot with anger that he could have fried bacon on his forehead. But there were four of them. And only one of him.

Maya pushed her wheels forward with shaking hands. Her eyes were shining, but her face was dry. Joseph couldn't let her get into trouble, not with these boys. Not tonight. Joseph grabbed the handles on the back of the chair and pulled it backward, fast. Maya barely got her hands off the wheels in time.

Then he ran, pushing the wheelchair past the people still coming to city hall and across another street.

He looked back, but the boys weren't following. Joseph rounded two more corners before he slowed down. When he finally stopped, Maya crossed her arms, her eyes narrowed to slits.

"I'm sorry, Maya," Joseph said, trying to catch his breath. "I couldn't fight them."

Maya let her face relax and shook her head. "I didn't expect you to fight them. I just wanted to call them something . . . mean. But we've got to finish our mission—no matter what stands in our way."

"You want to go back?" Joseph asked.

"You'd have to tie me up to keep me away," Maya said.

Joseph knew arguing wouldn't do any good now. And somehow, his anger had turned into a light feeling that made his heart want to float to the sky when he saw how strong Maya was.

Joseph and Maya made their way down the next block and then took the long way behind city hall. By the time they made it to the end of the alley, the line of people had mostly disappeared into the building. Only a few loitered around the entrance.

"It's now or never," Joseph said.

Joseph pushed the wheelchair against the wall of the alley and helped Maya to her feet so she could lean on him.

One step. Two steps. Three steps. Maya was already breathing hard, and Joseph was sweating.

Four steps.

Each step was agonizing, but they kept going, around the corner, down the sidewalk, and up to the front doors.

Fourteen, fifteen. They'd made it. They were at the front doors. But there were three men talking to Mrs. Bailey and blocking the entrance. Joseph kept his head down and tried to squeeze past. A hand landed on his shoulder.

"Where do you two kids think you're going?" asked Mrs. Bailey, her voice sweet as honey on a flytrap.

Joseph just tried to take another step.

"I'm sorry," said a man who stepped in front of Joseph, his pointy high-cut lace-up shoes firmly planted between them and the meeting. "We're all full. No more room."

Maya was getting heavier by the second. He could only hope she would keep her head down too.

No such luck.

"Mrs. Bailey," Maya said. Joseph could hear as her voice caught on the pain, but she kept going. "We need to speak at the meeting. We have to show them what the CCC camp has been doing."

Joseph finally looked up into the face of Mrs. Bailey. She towered over them in a flower-patterned dress, her curls pinned into a low chignon. There was no kindness there. She took the papers, the graphs, and charts that Maya had made of the pigeons.

"I know what the CCC camp has been doing," Mrs. Bailey said coldly. "Attacking innocent women. And you two were bystanders that day." She motioned to the man beside her. "Get them out of here."

And then to Joseph and Maya, she said, "You're not welcome."

The man grabbed Joseph. Maya's legs collapsed, but another man just lifted her by the arm and dragged her away from the door. The man who had Joseph tried to give him a shove, but Joseph was already two steps ahead of him, right beside Maya.

The doors shut behind them, leaving them alone on the sidewalk. One man stood in front of the door, guarding the entrance like a troll in front of his cave.

"Are you okay?" Joseph crouched down to inspect Maya.

"She took my papers," Maya said. "All of my work."

"We'll have to think of something else," Joseph said. "They're not going to let us in."

Maya hit the sidewalk with the palm of her hand. "It's not fair! None of this is fair! George didn't attack her. The camp is only trying to help."

"I know," Joseph said. "We'll just have to find a way to let people know. Maybe we could write the president."

Maya looked up at Joseph. "Or the First Lady."

Joseph nodded. "I'll go get your chair." Then he ran the fifteen steps back to the alley to get Maya's wheelchair.

But the chair was gone.

Chapter Seventeen

Joseph looked around frantically, but the alley was empty.

"Did you lose something?" The voice startled Joseph, and he looked to see where it was coming from. It was the boy with the light hair who had said Maya's legs looked like shriveled raisins. He and his friends had followed Maya and Joseph after all.

The boy dragged the wheelchair forward. The axle was bent, one of the wheels had fallen completely off, and the handles were broken and hung sideways.

"It really does belong in a junkyard." The boy tossed the loose wheel next to the broken chair. "You all belong in the junkyard," he spat.

Joseph clenched his fists. Earlier, Maya had wanted to call them something mean. Now Joseph wanted to do something much worse. Joseph ran toward the boys, but one of them brought out a stick he'd had behind his back and swung it at Joseph. It caught him in the shoulder, and Joseph fell to his knees.

"Go get the crippled one," the biggest boy said.

"No!" Joseph tried to get up but was pushed down again.

"Joseph!" Maya was close.

Joseph scrambled along the ground and threw himself over Maya. The boys stood over the two of them. The boy raised the stick again. Joseph closed his eyes and waited. He heard a dull *thunk*, but felt nothing.

He peeked through his eyelids and saw light glinting off fancy Bostonians.

Mr. Healey stood in front of the boys. He'd caught the stick in his hand and pulled it from the boy's hand.

"Hey, it's the crazy coot from the west side," said one of the boys.

Mr. Healey growled, deep as an animal, and stepped forward.

"Run!" It only took one of the boys to split, and the others were right on his tail.

Joseph pushed himself off Maya, and they both looked up at Mr. Healey.

"Why?" Joseph asked, unable to put together a full sentence.

Mr. Healey shrugged. "I came to see the meeting."

"It's not too late," Maya said, sitting up straighter, pointing up toward Mr. Healey. "You can get us in. You could get them to listen."

Mr. Healey shook his head. "I've already been in there. Only one person is getting a word in, and she's got the whole room ready for a riot. They've got a mob brewing in there. It's best if you get home."

Joseph looked at the broken chair up the alley and then at Maya. They'd made it fifteen steps, barely. How many steps was it back to the shop?

"I can help." Mr. Healey shifted his feet, almost as if he were uncomfortable. "If you'll let me."

Maya looked down, and Joseph thought she might argue. They hadn't even had a chance to help George, to remind people about the good work the CCC had done.

But Maya finally nodded, and Mr. Healey lifted Maya into his arms and started walking.

Joseph tried to pull the wheelchair along behind him, but one wheel wouldn't turn and the other wobbled. It was too heavy to drag. Mr. Healey wasn't slowing down, so Joseph was forced to leave the chair. Each time he glanced back, it disappeared farther into the shadows of the alley.

The chair was gone, and they hadn't made it into the meeting. Joseph was mad, and even though Mr. Healey was helping, watching those fancy shoes flash with each step made Joseph jumpy.

After two blocks, Joseph couldn't keep his questions in. "Why do you need two pairs of shoes?"

"*Two* pairs?" Mr. Healey almost sounded like he had more.

"I saw you pay Mrs. Jackson twenty-five dollars for a pair of shoes when you already had some on your feet."

"I buy shoes every month," Mr. Healey said. "With money the government borrowed. Borrowed money that gets passed around until it's more worthless than a pile of junk."

"If money lets you buy shoes," Joseph said, "it seems real enough to me."

"Why Mrs. Jackson?" Maya interrupted. Maya seemed to have missed the point. "Not too many folks from your side of town go in there. She's had to start trading to keep her store open, so I'm sure she is glad for the business."

Mr. Healey kept his eyes straight ahead, his mumbling getting loud for a minute and then getting quiet, like a wave that comes and goes.

Mr. Healey cleared his throat. "Mrs. Jackson's husband died in World War I," Mr. Healey finally answered. "He did braver things than I ever did. Never recognized here in the States. Another war hero forgotten. I just wanted to tell his widow thanks."

"By buying shoes?" Joseph didn't mean for his voice to squeak. He was just so tired of being confused. Why didn't anything make sense?

Mr. Healey stopped and looked up at the sky. "What else do you spend borrowed money on? When you can't stop them or make them see? When you're helpless?"

Joseph had no answer.

Maya thought for a moment and then said, "You're not helpless. You saved us. You're a hero."

Mr. Healey didn't answer, but Joseph noticed he walked with his back a little straighter, even with the weight of Maya in his arms.

ELSINORE DAILY CHRONICLE

CHAMBER OF COMMERCE GETS APPROVAL TO REMOVE LOCAL CCC CAMP

Official word came in yesterday that the CCC camp, Company 2923, is being relocated to Camp Yucca Creek, about 250 miles northwest of Elsinore, to work in the Sequoia National Park. The announcement was met with relief from some members of the community.

"There's nothing more important than protecting our children and providing a safe place for them to grow up," said Mrs. Shirley Bailey. "But despite the attack on my person, I'm glad those boys have work. And I'm glad it's far away from our beautiful town."

While there were some voices in favor of keeping the CCC camp for their contribution to firefighting and wilderness conservation, those voices were in the minority. The petition collected over 500 signatures in favor of relocating the CCC camp.

The relocation will happen by the end of the week.

Chapter Eighteen

The field lay empty, a few forgotten pieces of twine and dents in the earth the only evidence of a camp that had teamed with life a few days before.

Joseph had failed. He and Maya hadn't gotten into the chamber of commerce meeting. They hadn't been able to make a lick of difference. George was gone. The birds were gone. Maya's chair was broken. His world was as empty as the field.

Joseph had planned to see if he could get some shoeshine work today. After all, the camp—and his source of income—was gone. He used to be the best shoeshine in Elsinore. He didn't know what he was now. A terrible spy. And an even worse brother. Maya's legs were so sore after their attempt at city hall that she hadn't even tried to get out of bed the last three days.

Instead of going straight into town, Joseph had found his feet pulling him to the field, to the spot where the empty pigeon loft sat abandoned, the single door squeaking on its hinge in the wind.

George had promised to keep the pigeon training going—had even left Joseph a picture of the birds in their new loft. But it didn't matter anymore.

It had all been for nothing.

Joseph started to turn away, but he heard the familiar coo of a pigeon. He thought he was imagining things. But then the door flapped open, and Simon dropped into the loft in front of him!

Simon was back!

Joseph dropped his shoeshine box and it landed with a *thunk*. He reached in and carefully pulled Simon out, keeping the pigeon's wings pinned to its sides so Joseph could check the message carrier. He found a short note:

This one missed his friends. Take care of him for me. From, George.

Maya would be so happy! Joseph crossed the field and grabbed the old, bent cage they'd left behind the shop. He put Simon inside, excited to show Maya. But as he entered the shop, he knew something was wrong. Maya was sitting up in her bed, her fingers clenched around the edges of her thin mattress. Uncle Tanner was pacing by the stove.

When Joseph shut the door, Uncle Tanner whirled on him. "What are you doing back? Aren't you supposed to be out working? Getting us some food?"

Joseph held up the cage. "I just wanted to show Maya—"

Uncle Tanner swatted the cage from Joseph's hand, sending it crashing to the ground.

"No!" Maya yelled. She slipped out of bed, cringing as she landed on her hip, and pulled herself toward Simon.

Joseph dropped to his knees to make sure Simon was okay.

"Get up off the floor," Uncle Tanner said. Quiet. Dangerous. "You got two strong legs. Get up and use them. You're being held back."

Joseph couldn't take it anymore. Uncle Tanner couldn't even bother to say her name. Maya wasn't invisible. She wasn't embarrassing. She was his sister, and he wanted

Uncle Tanner to look at her. Sometimes spies had to lie, but sometimes the truth was more important.

Joseph stood up. "Maya isn't holding me back," he said, looking his uncle in the eyes. "Maya is smart and strong. She's twice the person you are!"

Uncle Tanner lunged forward and lifted Joseph up by the collar of his shirt, shaking him until Joseph's teeth rattled.

"Stop!" Maya yelled, trying to pull herself closer to Uncle Tanner.

"You don't talk to me that way!" Uncle Tanner yelled. "I've given you a roof over your head, a place to sleep and keep warm. This is the respect you show me?"

Maya reached Uncle Tanner and wrapped herself around his leg. Joseph saw her open her mouth and bite down on Uncle Tanner's calf.

Uncle Tanner dropped Joseph, a roar coming out of his mouth as he lifted his hand to hit Maya. His eyes fell on Maya, and hand in the air, he looked at her for the first time in months. Joseph jumped up to catch Uncle Tanner's arm, but the hand didn't fall. Uncle Tanner's eyes widened, and his breath caught, like he'd been splashed with a bucket of water.

Uncle Tanner stepped back and crossed his arms over his head, his face buried in the crooks of his elbows.

Then he ran to his room and slammed the door.

Neither Joseph nor Maya said anything as Maya crawled back toward the bed. They listened to the sobs as Uncle Tanner cried for the first time since Joseph had known him.

Much later that night, Joseph lay in the dark, unable to fall asleep. He had stayed with Maya all day, but tomorrow he'd go to town and shine some shoes. He'd find a way to fix this.

Suddenly, a thought hit him. His shoeshine box! He'd been so excited about Simon he'd left it out in the field.

Quietly, so as not to wake Maya, Joseph slipped out the door and made his way around the shop in the dark. The field was a graveyard of shadows and memories. Joseph kept one hand in front of him and made his way toward the dark shape of the loft. When he reached the loft, he felt around for his shoeshine box.

As he bent to lift the wood handle, Joseph noticed a line of lights curling across the horizon.

There wasn't a town in that direction. No roads either. Joseph squinted. Yellow lights dancing on the edge of the mountain.

Fire! The mountains were on fire!

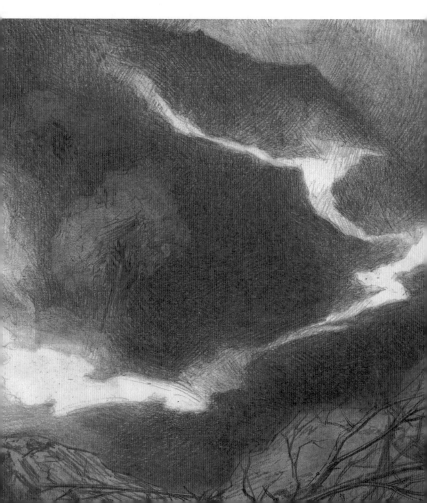

Chapter Nineteen

Joseph watched the flickering for a moment, realization dawning slowly. The fire had come. And the CCC camp was gone.

The people in town would have to fight the fire on their own.

Unless . . .

Joseph stumbled across the field in the dark, tripping on the uneven ground. He had to send Simon to get help. Simon hadn't been trained to fly away from the CCC camp, only to come back, but Mr. Healey had said a pigeon could fly between two locations. Maybe, if miracles happened, Simon would find his way back to George.

In the shop, Joseph turned on the single light bulb and looked around frantically for a piece of paper and pencil. He had to write a message.

"What are you doing?" Maya sat up, rubbing her eyes.

"There's a fire on the mountain," Joseph said, finally finding Maya's plans for her wheelchair. "We have to tell George." He ripped off the corner of the paper and found a pencil. Maya was just sitting up, rubbing her eyes.

"George?" Maya asked. "The town made them leave. Why would they come back?"

Joseph closed his eyes and took a breath. "George said they would come."

Maya's mouth opened, but she just nodded. "Here. Let me write it. You go get Simon." Joseph handed the pencil and scrap of paper to Maya. Then he went and got Simon out of the cage, attaching the message carrier. Maya's note read:

Fire coming for Elsinore. South of the shop. Please come quick. J & M.

Joseph stepped back outside, Simon in his hands.

"You've got to fly to George," Joseph said. "Bring him back."

Joseph opened his hands, and Simon flew up into the air, turning into a speck of gray against the black night. Joseph watched until Simon disappeared between the stars.

The breeze brushed against his face, smelling of smoke.

Back inside, Joseph pulled Maya up and tried to keep her arms wrapped around his neck, but her grip was weak, and her legs wouldn't hold her. Maya slipped onto the floor. Frustration brought tears to Joseph's eyes, and he turned away so Maya wouldn't see.

"It's okay," Maya said. She sat against her bed. "I'll be okay. Simon will find them. Go help fight the fire."

"I'm not leaving without you."

Just then, Uncle Tanner burst through the front door. "I was looking everywhere!" He sounded out of breath. "I thought you'd run away." Uncle Tanner knelt on the floor in front of them, looking straight at Maya. "I've been wrong, and I'm sorry. You two are stronger than me, and that's hard for a man to accept. Can you forgive me?"

Maya reached up and placed a hand on the side of Uncle Tanner's face. "We were just waiting for you to come around."

Uncle Tanner stood to help Maya up and put her back in bed.

"Wait," Maya said. "There's a fire coming."

"Fire?" Uncle Tanner must not have seen it. "We better wake up the town. The hills are as dry as bone. A wildfire will spread quickly."

"I'll get Mrs. Jackson," Joseph said. "She'll help me wake up the mayor."

"I'll take Maya," Uncle Tanner said, shifting her higher so she could get her arms around his neck.

"I've missed you," Maya said, burying her head against his broad shoulder.

"I'm so sorry," Uncle Tanner whispered. "You were here the whole time, and I just didn't let myself see."

Joseph ran to Mrs. Jackson's mercantile. She slept in a room at the back of her store, and Joseph pounded on the door until she came out.

"The mountains are on fire!" Joseph shouted.

"Lord have mercy!" Mrs. Jackson grabbed a shawl beside her door, and they both hurried down the street.

The next few hours were a whirlwind of chaos, men yelling, sirens blaring, feet running back and forth, some with shoes, some without. Joseph wished for the order of the CCC camp—men in straight lines, following orders.

Even when they finally had a group of men and women gathered with shovels in front of city hall, everyone was trying to yell over one other. No one seemed to know which way to go.

Finally, Joseph yelled at the top of his lungs, "It's coming from the south!"

The noise settled down, people turning their heads to see where the words had come from. Joseph kept his head down, small in the crowd, a spy and a messenger.

"We need to make a fire break." Joseph moved to another spot in the crowd, making sure his voice carried. "Head south."

Joseph heard his words repeated as the message was passed through the crowd. It was Mr. Healey's voice at first, then others joined in. Mr. Healey was here to help fight the fire. Enough of the crowd was antsy for direction that a large group moved toward the street that led to Uncle Tanner's shop without questioning who was giving orders.

Slipping through the bodies, Joseph walked alongside Mr. Healey.

"I sent out the bird," Joseph told him.

Mr. Healey nodded. "Now we just have to see if they come."

They reached the field and moved past it, some people moving to the sides of the road while others headed into the brush. Joseph followed Mr. Healey to a row of tall, dry sagebrush and dug in his shovel.

Joseph watched as the fire moved down the mountain, a small string of lights that flickered on the black horizon and grew larger with each passing minute. More minutes—or maybe it was hours—passed as Joseph worked, ash falling from the sky, landing on his hair and arms like gray snowflakes. Men dug and picked at the ground around him. Once or twice, a water truck drove by, drenching the land and men alike.

The fire got closer, and Joseph couldn't tell if dawn was on the horizon or if the flames were lighting the sky. Joseph was exhausted. His feet were scraped and bleeding from the times he'd hit them with the shovel in the dark. His back hurt, and his arms felt like rubber. He had several blisters on his hands, but still he dug.

Dawn did come, blues and pinks and purples along the burned and blackened mountain skyline. Smoke columned into the sky, blocking the sun as it tried to make an entrance.

"Look how fast she's moving." Mr. Healey's voice held awe and a slight tremor of fear. "We can't stop it. There aren't enough of us."

Joseph's heart sunk low. Would the whole town of Elsinore go up in flames?

Just then, a rumbling sound vibrated through the air, shaking the ground under Joseph's feet. Joseph turned slowly, wondering if he'd somehow fallen asleep while digging and was now lost in a dream. Because there, coming down the road, was a line of CCC trucks, loaded down with the black workers who had been forced out of town.

Heroes, coming to save them.

Chapter Twenty

Henry,

I'm not much for writing letters. Nor for sentiment. You did what you thought was right. You made a choice. And it was a good one.

I worked side by side with some of your boys. Watching them work, imagining you being like that, strong, confident, heroes in every way. They saved our town yesterday. Fought a fire to save people who didn't even want them around.

That's the kind of people this world needs. People like you.

I'm mighty proud.

Your father,
Kimball Healey

"Shoeshine!" Joseph called as the men hurried past. "Get your shoeshine! I'm the best shoeshine in Elsinore City!"

A pair of goodyear welts stopped in front of him, and Joseph pulled out his cleaning supplies. The fire had been put out; the only building that had burned had been a barn a mile outside the city limits. The fire had come all the way up to the edge of the field, but the CCC workers had dug a line so quickly that the fire had no way to come any closer. Then they had fought to put out every last spark. It had taken seven days of CCC workers and Elsinore citizens working together.

Now there was a new feeling in town, kind of like the air right after a rainstorm. No one had apologized, and the CCC camp hadn't moved back, but Joseph was getting business again. Uncle Tanner had even gotten a job as a machinist at the new orange juice factory in town.

That might mean Joseph would have to head back to school, but he wasn't quite ready yet.

It wasn't until he finished the shoeshine that Joseph realized another pair of shoes were waiting next to him.

Star lace-ups. Mrs. Jackson. She never closed her shop in the middle of the day.

Joseph looked up.

"There's a new item at the store. I was wondering if you could come help me deliver it," Mrs. Jackson asked.

"Sure," Joseph said, pocketing his money from the goodyear welts and following her back to the mercantile. He would have charged anyone else a nickel, but not Mrs. Jackson. Just in case she really had outwitted a mobster, he wanted to stay on her good side.

But when Joseph walked into the mercantile, his jaw might as well have dropped all the way to the floor. There, in the center of the store, was a brand-new wheelchair—metal bars, padded seat, the works. Probably as fancy as President Roosevelt's.

"Where did you get that?" Joseph asked.

"Someone came in with a lot of new shoes. Said he wanted to trade them in for something more . . . valuable." Mrs. Jackson's mouth didn't smile, but her eyes danced just a little.

"Mr. Healey?" Joseph asked. "But—but—"

Mrs. Jackson walked behind her counter and straightened the penny candy. "I think the shoes were just something that distracted him from what was really important."

Joseph couldn't believe it.

"You better get that present on home to Maya," Mrs. Jackson said.

"Yes, ma'am." Joseph pushed the chair forward, amazed that it fit right through the door.

It only took a few minutes to get home. Joseph couldn't wait to see the look on Maya's face.

As Joseph rolled the wheelchair inside, he passed Simon's cage.

Simon pecked at the wires, ready for his next mission.

Author's Note

This is a fictional story, but many of the characters are inspired by actual people, and many of the events are based on actual things that happened during the Great Depression.

While many Americans suffered from unemployment and meager finances during this time, others did not. There was construction, movies, fashion, and inventions that those with jobs and financial security could enjoy. But others lived very different lives.

To start, class division increased between the rich and the poor. There were hundreds of strikes during the Great Depression as workers fought for better working conditions and pay. When CCC camps were first formed, many people were afraid they would take jobs away from locals, but the program proved beneficial for many communities and remained popular through 1942.

The racial divide widened across the nation during the Depression as people fought for the few jobs that were available. In this story, Joseph experienced this when the townspeople refused to give him work shining their shoes.

And Uncle Tanner's situation was similar to hundreds of African Americans, who had an unemployment rate of 30 to 50 percent higher than whites during the Great Depression. Not only were there physical difficulties with being unemployed for such extended periods of time, but there were also severe psychological effects.

Despite discrimination being against national CCC policy, there were problems from the start of the New Deal. The number of African Americans in the CCC was capped at 10 percent of total enrollment based on population, but many states refused to let black people enroll at all until the government threatened to close the program. Although some states segregated camps earlier, in July 1935, CCC National Director Robert Fechner instructed all camps to segregate nationwide.

The contribution of the segregated camps has been overlooked and often ignored. Among other difficult projects, Company 2923-C, one of the five segregated camps in California, raised and trained pigeons to fly to fire-suppression camps when other communication was unavailable. They were the first company in the United

States to use homing pigeons as a fire-warning system. The character George was inspired by Robert D'Hue, an African American artist who served in Company 2923-C.

The actual timeline was crunched for convenience in the story. The segregation of camps in California took place in August 1935. Company 2923-C actually remained at Camp la Cienega near Elsinore, California, for three years, where they raised and trained pigeons. This company fought several major forest fires in 1935, including the Malibu Mountain and Brown Mountain fires. In 1938, the company moved to Camp San Pablo. It was here that Company 2923-C experienced community harassment and intimidation, and moved to Camp Yucca Creek.

The story of the pigeon Cher Ami, told by Mr. Healey, is a true account of a messenger pigeon during World War I. During the Meuse-Argonne Offensive, in October 1918, Cher Ami delivered the message to the American headquarters despite being severely wounded, saving the lives of 194 soldiers. Cher Ami was awarded several medals for bravery and was inducted into the Pigeon Racing Hall of Fame.

Mr. Healey represents those veterans who were part of the smaller Bonus Army that marched at the beginning of President Roosevelt's term as president. The Bonus Army originally marched in 1932; over 43,000 protesters requested that their promised bonuses from the World War Adjusted Compensation Act of 1924 be paid early. Most of the veterans had been out of work since the beginning of the Depression, and their bonus certificates could not be redeemed until 1945. The protestors were removed by the army in 1932 and denied again by President Roosevelt in 1933.

Maya's struggles with paralysis from polio represent the thousands of people affected by the disease in the early twentieth century. Polio vaccines were not successfully developed until the 1950s. During the 1920s, the scientific community considered polio a "white disease" and believed that blacks were not susceptible. In 1944, the March of Dimes worked to educate and counteract these incorrect beliefs to get help and resources to all children suffering from the effects of polio.

The story of Joseph McCoy and his involvement in the raising and training of the pigeons is fictional. Every human experience is unique, and each of us can find a way to learn about and understand people who've come before us, the legacy they've left us, and the connection we all have to each other.

Photos

Shoeshine boys in 1939 Waco, Texas. Notice how the boy on the right does not wear any shoes, just like Joseph in this story.

Civilian Conservation Corps Camp Skokie Valley Company 605, Illinois, 1939

The US Army raised pigeons to deliver messages during World War I.

CCC workers help to control a fire near Angeles National Forest in California.

Civilian Conservation Corps

The Civilian Conservation Corps was the most popular of President Roosevelt's New Deal programs. By 1942, the CCC had employed more than 3 million men and 8,500 women.

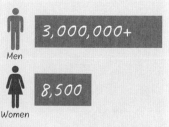

Men 3,000,000+

Women 8,500

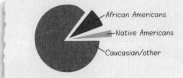

African Americans

Native Americans

Caucasian/other

250,000 of those were African American, and 80,000 were Native American.

Despite national policy against racial discrimination, due to racial fears and biases, some states segregated the CCC camps from the beginning. California created five segregated camps in August 1935 when the CCC was segregated on a national level. The CCC remained segregated until its end in 1942. There were a total of 4,500 CCC camps during the duration of the program, costing the government $3 billion.

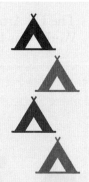

The CCC planted over 2.5 billion trees for reforestation. They developed new firefighting methods, built over 3,000 lookout towers, and had over 8 million firefighting hours. The CCC strung over 89,000 miles of telephone wires and built over 300,000 check dams for erosion control. The CCC built thousands of miles of roads and trails that we still use today in hundreds of state and national parks.

African Americans in California during the Great Depression

In 1930, 1.4 percent of California's population of 5,677,251 were African American.

African Americans in Los Angeles, California, had the highest unemployment rate of any racial group during the Great Depression. The proportion of blacks who were unemployed was 30 to 50 percent greater than whites during the same period.

1933 was the worst unemployment year of the Great Depression, with over 14,762,000 known unemployed and over one-third of those under the age of 25.

Pigeon Facts

During World War I, when communication systems were still being developed, over 100,000 pigeons were used to deliver messages with a 95 percent success rate.

There are many theories about how pigeons navigate, from a magnetic compass to their sense of smell.

About the Author

Tracy Daley has helped refine and edit dozens of books throughout her career. She has held many positions in publishing, including editor, publicity specialist, and acquisitions editor. She lives with her husband and three kids in Taylorsville, Utah, but escapes to the mountains as often as possible.

About the Consultant

Andrew Lee Feight, PhD, is a Professor of American History at Shawnee State University in Portsmouth, Ohio. He is the winner of the Kentucky Historical Society's 2005 Richard H. Collins Award. His current research focuses on the history of African Americans in the Civilian Conservation Corps.

About the Illustrator

Eric Freeberg has illustrated over twenty-five books for children, and has created work for magazines and ad campaigns. He was a winner of the 2010 London Book Fair's Children's Illustration Competition; the 2010 Holbein Prize for Fantasy Art, International Illustration Competition, Japan Illustrators' Association; Runner-Up, 2013 SCBWI Magazine Merit Award; Honorable Mention, 2009 SCBWI Don Freeman Portfolio Competition; and 2nd Prize, 2009 Clymer Museum's Annual Illustration Invitational. He was also a winner of the Elizabeth Greenshields Foundation Award.

History is full of storytellers

Take a sneak peek at an excerpt from
Journey to a Promised Land: A Story of the Exodusters
by Allison Lassieur, another story from the
I Am America series.

◆

April 5, 1879
Dear Diary,

We had a spelling bee at school today. Me and
Josephine were tied for first at the end. Then
Miss Banneker gave us the hardest word.
Chrysanthemum. I did right terrible with it. I lost
my head after the "R." Jo got it right though. I'd
have been mad if she weren't my best friend. But
it's important that I get my spelling right if I am to
become a teacher. Oh my! I can't believe I just wrote
that down. It's a good thing Bram can't read yet
because I haven't told that secret to anyone. But it
is my deepest desire . . .

Hattie

It was one of those late-spring days when the world is bright and warm, and everything feels possible. Hattie ran the ten crowded blocks from the First Baptist AME Church toward home, her heart pounding hard from excitement or the running, she wasn't sure which. She expertly dodged the dirty pools of water in the street, weaved past the butcher's store that always smelled of blood, and ducked into a narrow alley. It was crisscrossed with a web of clotheslines that dipped heavily with the laundry her mother took in for extra money.

Hattie stopped short, breathing heavily. "Mama!" she called. "I'm home!"

"In the back, baby," came her mother's voice.

Mama was bent over an enormous black iron cauldron, pushing a wooden paddle back and forth in the bubbling, gray water. The familiar scents of wood smoke, lye soap, and steamy clothes hung in the air. She saw Hattie and paused in her work, smiling.

Hattie threw her arms around her mother in a quick hug, feeling those thin, strong arms wrapped around her like a comforting blanket.

"Mama, guess what? Miss Banneker picked me for the recital! I'm going to read a poem in front of everybody!"

Mama beamed with pride. Her rough hand, cracked and hardened through years of work, stroked Hattie's cheek. "Oh, baby, I'm so proud of you," she said.

"Will you come?" Hattie asked, still out of breath from the run. She knew what the answer would be, but she asked anyway, just to hear it.

"I wouldn't miss it for the world," her mother replied. "Papa too. And Abraham, if we can keep him from squirming through the whole thing."

Hattie grinned. She knew how much stock her parents put on learning. When they were enslaved, they hadn't been allowed to learn to read or write. After the Civil War, one of the first things they'd both done was go to school.

"Speaking of your papa, he needs his lunch, and you do too. It's on the table."

Another hug and Hattie dashed through the narrow doorway at the end of the alley. She took the rickety stairs two at a time up to their small two-room apartment. The front room served as kitchen and dining room. The black iron cook stove took up most of the space, along with a table and chairs. The back room held the big, soft bed for

Mama and Papa. Hidden beneath it was the trundle bed for Hattie and Abraham.

Every day when school let out at noon, Hattie came home to take Papa his lunch. Mama always had the food carefully wrapped and waiting. Hattie grabbed the packet and sniffed. Biscuits and sausage, Hattie's favorite.

"Bye, Mama!" she called. But Mama was bent over the tub again, wearily wiping sweat and steam from her forehead.

———————◆———————

Want to read what happens next?

Check out
Journey to a Promised Land: A Story of the Exodusters

Explore More Stories from History

JOURNEY TO A PROMISED LAND

◆

A Story of the Exodusters

By Allison Lassieur
Illustrated by Eric Freeberg

Hattie Jacobs has a secret dream: to go to school to become a teacher. But her parents were formerly enslaved and are struggling to survive in Nashville, Tennessee, after Reconstruction. When the Jacobs family joins the Great Exodus of 1879 to Kansas, their journey in search of a better life is filled with danger and hardship. Will they make it to the Mississippi River unharmed? What will be waiting for them in Kansas, and will it live up to their dreams?

"This well-written volume fills a major gap in historical fiction."
—*Kirkus Reviews*, starred review

Hardcover ISBN: 978-1-63163-275-4
Paperback ISBN: 978-1-63163-276-1

LINES WE DRAW

A Story of Imprisoned Japanese Americans

By Camellia Lee
Illustrated by Eric Freeberg

It's August 1941 when Sumiko Adachi starts at a new school in Phoenix, Arizona. In spite of her first-day jitters, she finds a friendly face in Emi Kuno. But everything changes after Japan bombs Pearl Harbor, and the United States enters World War II. Suddenly the girls are faced with anti-Japanese sentiment from classmates and neighbors. When an arbitrary dividing line is drawn through Phoenix, the girls find themselves

on opposite sides. Can Sumiko and Emi maintain their friendship when one of them is forced into a confinement camp, and the other is allowed to remain free?

Hardcover ISBN: 978-1-63163-279-2
Paperback ISBN: 978-1-63163-280-8

UNITED TO STRIKE

A Story of the Delano Grape Workers

By Molly Zenk
Illustrated by Eric Freeberg

Budding reporter Tala Mendoza thinks life in 1965 Delano, California, is boring. But that's before her father and other members of the local Filipino grape workers' union vote to strike. While the strike brings Filipino and Mexican farmworkers together, it threatens to tear Tala and her best friend, Jasmine, apart. Can Tala and Jasmine's relationship withstand the strain and length of the Delano Grape Strike?

Hardcover ISBN: 978-1-63163-283-9
Paperback ISBN: 978-1-63163-284-6

OCT   2019